BA

Clint Adams found out then that the three of them were pretty fast in their own right. As he pulled his gun, the leader suddenly kicked out, catching him on the wrist. His hand went numb as the gun spun through the air away from all of them.

Now Clint found out what the third man had behind his back as a long knife came into view. It had a smooth, slender blade, and the Gunsmith could see that it was razor-sharp.

The three of them closed on him, and Clint knew he wasn't going to come out of this without some damage—if he came out of it at all . . .

* * *

SPECIAL PREVIEW!

Turn to the back of this book for an exciting look at a new epic trilogy . . .

Northwest Destiny

. . . the sprawling saga of brotherhood, pride, and rage on the American frontier.

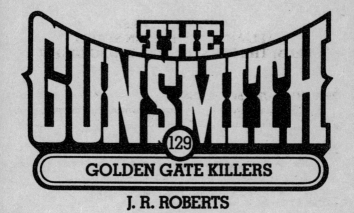

THE GUNSMITH

129

GOLDEN GATE KILLERS

J. R. ROBERTS

JOVE BOOKS, NEW YORK

GOLDEN GATE KILLERS

A Jove Book / published by arrangement with
the author

PRINTING HISTORY
Jove edition / September 1992

ISBN: 0-515-10931-2

Jove Books are published by The Berkley Publishing Group,
200 Madison Avenue, New York, New York 10016.
The name "JOVE" and the "J" logo
are trademarks belonging to Jove Publications, Inc.

PRINTED IN THE UNITED STATES OF AMERICA

10 9 8 7 6 5 4 3 2 1

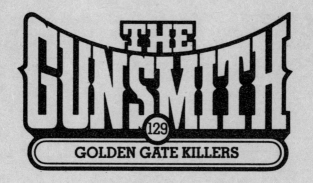

THE GUNSMITH

129

GOLDEN GATE KILLERS

PROLOGUE

Clint Adams looked across the table at Luke Short, hoping to read something in the man's eyes that would tell him whether he had that flush he seemed to be betting so confidently. He should have known better, though, because as many years as he knew the little gambler, he'd never known the man to exhibit any kind of a gambler's "tell"—a movement, facial or otherwise, that would reveal something about the hand he was playing.

There were four hearts sitting on the table in front of Luke Short, and whether his down card was a fifth one was something only he knew and everyone else had to pay to find out.

Even Clint Adams.

Clint didn't need to look at his down card to know what he had. He had an up and down straight on the table in front of him, ranging from nine to queen, and his down card was a king. He *had* his straight, but if Short *had* his flush, then Clint's hand was second best—and second best never won anything, not in this game.

There was a considerable amount of money in the pot,

1

because this was a big game. It was a game that came to town only twice a year, and was played in a hotel room at the Alhambra Hotel in Portsmouth Square. Certain people had an open invitation to this game, people like Clint, and Luke Short, and some of the other people who were now sitting at the table waiting for Clint to make his play. Among them were Bat Masterson, Harry "the Deuce" Walker, and Dominick Asher, a gambler who had been riding a "hot hand" for several months—until this game had started the night before.

There were five other people in the game, which made a total of ten players. The *only* game they played was five-card stud—"real poker," as some of them called it.

Usually *more than* ten players showed up, but the first ten to arrive got a chair, while the others had to wait for a chair to empty before they could play. Since this was only the second night of the game, there was no danger of that happening anytime soon.

Others at the table were Johnny Lutz, Jerry Healy, and Tommy Ross, who were more or less semiregulars on the circuit. There were only two totally unknown quantities seated at the table at the present time, and they had come with letters of introduction. They were Bob McCoy and a smoothie by the name of Les Roberts.

At the moment, however, the only two players left in *this* particular hand were Clint and Luke Short. Short had been the big winner the first night, and for the past hour had continued that pace.

His luck had to end sometime.

"I'll call," Clint said, and threw two hundred dollars into the pot.

"I thought you might," Short said, and turned over an ace—a *black* ace. It gave him a pair of aces.

No flush.

Clint turned over his king, showing everyone that he had the straight.

It was a good pot for Clint, one of the few he had taken

since the game had started the night before.

"Maybe your luck is changing for the better," Johnny Lutz said as he gathered up the cards for the next deal, which was his.

Clint looked at Lutz and said, "That's the only way it *could* change."

When the game broke up late that evening Luke Short and Bat Masterson approached Clint with an offer of a late dinner.

"Sure," Clint said. "Why not? You two have all the money."

As the game continued that week there would be nights when it wouldn't break up at all, just continue on into the morning, but it was still early for that kind of intensity.

Clint, Short, and Masterson went down to the Alhambra dining room and took a table that Short had reserved for the length of his stay in San Francisco. It was a corner table, and afforded the diner a view of the entire room. It bordered two walls, and Short and Clint took them for their backs. Masterson sat with his left side to the room and a wall on his right. Normally his gun would have been on his right hip, but while he was in San Francisco he would be wearing it in a shoulder rig. Short had a holster sewn into the lining of his jacket, and wore his gun there. Clint shunned a shoulder rig and wore his gun on his hip. There were times he wore a rig, but he found them uncomfortable, and when he was playing cards he wanted to be comfortable.

"You still staying over at the Silver Spur?" Short asked him.

"Yep." The Silver Spur was a hotel just outside the vaunted Portsmouth Square, where all the "big" hotels and casinos were. Clint had stayed there several months ago, before he was drafted into service tracking down a stolen gold shipment from Caliente to Mexico. He had liked it so much that when he came to San Francisco for the poker game, he decided to stay there again. The owner, Terence

White, and he had become quite friendly.

"Why not move to one of the larger hotels?" Masterson asked.

"I like the Spur," he said. "I get treated well there."

"How's the food?" Short asked.

"Not as good as here," Clint said, "but then I can't eat this rich *every* night."

A waitress came over, a pretty thing in her twenties who had waited on Short the night before. On this night, however, she had eyes only for Bat Masterson, who graced her with a smile.

"What can I get you?" she asked, looking directly at him.

Masterson exchanged amused glances with his colleagues and said, "A steak will do for now, with some vegetables, and a cold beer."

Clint and Short ordered the same, and the girl went off to get them.

"I've got twenty dollars says Bat gets the biggest steak," Short said.

"No bet," Clint said.

"The man has an uncanny way with waitresses," Short said. "I've never seen the like, but I get the best service I'll ever get when I sit with him."

Bat accepted the good-natured ribbing in the spirit that it was given and smiled.

Not yet thirty, Bat said to Short, "You probably did well enough with women when you were younger, Luke."

"When I was younger?" Short, a year older than Masterson, repeated. "Why, you young pup . . ."

Clint, older than both of them by some years, sat back and enjoyed their good-natured banter. He knew both men fairly well, and indeed counted both as friends. However, he sensed that he had been invited to dine with them for a reason, and he was curious as to what it was. And so he interrupted them.

"Excuse me, gents, but I assume I was invited to dinner for a reason," Clint said, "and I'd like to know what it is."

Short and Masterson exchanged a glance, and it was Short

who said, "Couldn't it have been for the pleasure of your company?"

Clint grinned.

"Most of the time I'm sure that's the reason, Luke," Clint said, "but I have a feeling that this isn't one of those times."

"The man is uncanny," Bat Masterson said, smiling at Short. Obviously, then, it was Short who wanted to ask Clint something, and Bat found it amusing that Clint had seen through the invitation to dinner. It wasn't as though they never had dinner together, but not often while they were playing poker in this big a game.

Clint took a moment to study his two companions. Both were splendidly dressed, each wearing a dark suit that cost more than he spent on an entire wardrobe. Both men were known as fine dressers, excellent poker players, and dangerous men with a gun—not in that order. They both sported well-cared-for, bushy mustaches, and affected bowlers rather than the more common flat-brimmed Stetson.

"Well, all right, I did invite you for a reason, Clint."

"Which is?"

"I have a friend here in San Francisco who is concerned about his son."

"What's the boy done?"

"He's, ah, gotten himself involved with a woman—a Chinese woman."

Clint remained silent, waiting for Short to continue at his own pace.

"He's looking for someone to, uh, look into the girl's, uh, situation."

"This man is wealthy, I imagine."

"He is."

"Why do you assume that?" Masterson asked.

Clint looked at Bat.

"Wealthy men are the only ones who want to 'look into someone's situation.' "

Clint had been quite right. Short had been using his friend's exact words.

Clint looked back at Short and said, "He's afraid the girl is after his money."

"Right again."

"He needs a detective."

"He asked for you."

"You didn't recommend me?" Clint asked, surprised that the 'wealthy man' had been the one to bring up his name.

"I did not," Short said. "He knew I was in town to play in the game, and he also knew that you played in it."

Clint frowned.

"How did he know that?"

"That's something you'll have to ask him."

"If I talk to him."

"Uh, that's right, if you talk to him. It could mean a lot of money for you, Clint."

"It's not the kind of thing I usually do," Clint said.

"I told him that," Short said.

"What else did you tell him?"

"I told him I would relay the message, and his address, to you, but that I would exert no influence to try to get you to accept his offer."

"You wouldn't *have* any influence," Clint pointed out.

"Yes, well, there is that."

When the silence at the table grew deafening, Short said, "Uh, do you want his address?"

"No," Clint said.

"Oh, I—"

"What's his name?"

"Wentworth, Samuel Wentworth."

The name meant nothing to Clint.

"Have him come to the Spur tomorrow morning," Clint said. "I'll see him there."

"Oh, well, all right. I suppose he could do that. . . ."

"If he wants me that bad," Clint said, "he'll have to, won't he?"

"I suppose—" Short began, but at that moment the waitress approached with their orders.

After she had put all three plates down and then fetched the beers, she smiled at Bat Masterson and said, "Will there be anything else?"

"No, that's all for now," Bat said. He didn't give her a smile or look at her this time, and she went away unhappy.

"Well," Short said to Clint, "I'm lucky you didn't take my bet."

"What bet was that?" Clint asked.

"That Bat would get the largest steak," Short said. "You seem to have gotten it."

Clint looked at his steak and then said, "Yes, I have, haven't I."

ONE

Sam Highbinder enjoyed a singular privilege.

At eighteen, working as a busboy in the Silver Spur Hotel—
which was just off Portsmouth Square—it was Highbinder
who had the privilege of holding Clint Adams's confidence—
to some extent.

Over the past few weeks, while Clint had been staying at the
hotel, whenever anyone came to the hotel and wanted to talk to
him, it was Highbinder who usually knew where he was—if he
was, indeed, in the hotel at the time. It also fell to Highbinder
to carry the news to Clint. That meant that whether Clint was
dining, resting, playing cards, or entertaining, Highbinder was
allowed to interrupt him—and *only* Highbinder was allowed
to interrupt him. It had been that way when Clint had been at
the hotel before, and even more so this trip.

The man who was standing at the front desk asking for Clint
looked like money to Highbinder.

"If you'll wait here, sir," he said to the man. "I'll tell Mr.
Adams that you're here."

"Thank you," the man said stiffly. He seemed out of place
in the hotel lobby. Although the Silver Spur boasted a fine

ambience—crystal and leather and fine wood—it was not as fancy as some of the hotels that were actually *in* Portsmouth Square, and this man seemed to know it and almost resent it.

"What was your name again, sir?" Sam Highbinder asked.

"My name is Wentworth," the man said, "Samuel Wentworth."

Highbinder, a native of San Francisco, recognized the name.

"Wentworth," Highbinder repeated, "yes, sir. I'll tell him."

"It probably won't mean anything to him," Wentworth said. "Just tell him that Luke Short suggested I come by to see him."

Luke Short! Now, *that* name meant something to Highbinder, as well.

"Yes, *sir,* I'll surely tell him."

Highbinder left the man in the lobby and went up to Clint's room, where he was sure Clint would still be at this time of the morning. Clint was usually an early riser, but sometimes rose late when he had been playing poker the night before.

Highbinder knew he'd been playing in the big game at the Alhambra, with Bat Masterson and Luke Short, among others.

Highbinder wondered if he could get Clint to introduce him to Masterson and Short while they were here.

Clint opened his eyes when the knocking started on the door. He rolled over to check the time, saw that it was not yet 9:00 A.M., and so knew that it was probably Sam Highbinder at the door. Even so, he couldn't help but be a little annoyed as he staggered naked to the door.

When he opened the door and glowered down at young Sam Highbinder, the youngster held his ground admirably. There was something about Highbinder that reminded Clint of himself at that age—not that he'd ever tell young Highbinder that.

"What is it?"

"A man to see you, Clint."

"Who?"

"Fella named Wentworth, *Samuel* Wentworth." Highbinder leaned closer and said in a low voice, "*Sam* Wentworth is worth plenty, Clint!"

"Don't know him."

"He said you probably wouldn't," Highbinder said. "Said to tell you that Luke Short suggested he come by to see you."

It all came back to him then. The dinner with Luke Short and Bat Masterson, and Short's talk of a friend with a problem.

"All right," Clint said, scratching his crotch, "take him into the dining room and put him at my table, give him some coffee, and tell the cook to get my breakfast ready."

"Eggs today?"

"Yeah, eggs and everything."

"All right."

"I'll be down in about fifteen minutes."

"I'll tell him."

There was a moan behind Clint, and Highbinder leaned over just far enough to see the naked woman in Clint's bed. Clint turned and looked at her. The moan reminded him that she was there. She was a willowy brunette he had met at the Alhambra last night, and brought back to the room with him. He'd forgotten about her.

"Make that twenty minutes," he said to Highbinder.

Highbinder grinned, and Clint shut the door in the grin.

After making the brunette moan some more—not to mention groan, squeak, and nearly scream—Clint poured some water into a basin and washed the sleep from his eyes, then used a washcloth on his body. He didn't have time for a leisurely bath, but maybe later tonight, before the game.

"That's a whore's bath," the woman on the bed said.

"I know," Clint said, wondering how *she* knew. "I don't have time for much more."

She got up on her knees and stared at him lasciviously. Her breasts were small, but they were high and firm, with remarkably responsive nipples that were once again hardening. She lifted her hands and cupped her breasts, touching her own nipples with her thumbs. Last night, at the Alhambra, all dressed up she had looked like a real lady, but once they had gotten to bed, she had turned into a tiger. Now, hair tousled, tweaking her own nipples, she had a slutty quality that made his groin tingle.

"Bring your body over here, Clint, and I'll wash it for you," she said, licking her lips to make her point clearer still.

"I would," he said, wanting to say her name but not remembering it, "but I've got someone waiting for me downstairs."

"Someone more interesting than me?"

"Definitely not," he said, reaching for his clothes, "but someone a damn sight richer."

On the way downstairs he thought about the game.

Things had not gone real well for him the first two nights, and as much as he hated taking on a job during the game, it might be advisable to do so now, especially if Short's friend were as wealthy as he said.

As he dressed he thought about as much as Short had been able to tell him. If a Chinese girl was after this Wentworth's son for his money, Clint would have been surprised—unless the girl was working for Toy Lee. He was going to have to go down to Ross Alley to see old Toy about this.

Fully dressed, he went to his chest of drawers and opened the top drawer. From it he extracted a rosewood case and opened it to reveal two .41-caliber Colt New Line pistols lying on a bed of red velvet. They had been a gift to him recently by a woman he'd helped out of a bad situation. He hadn't used them yet, but since he didn't intend to leave the hotel, he didn't want to wear his Colt. Still, he wouldn't even go to breakfast unarmed. He picked up one of the nickel-plated Derringers, enjoying the way the pearl handle felt in his hand. He loaded the pistol and dropped it into the side pocket of his jacket, then went down for breakfast.

TWO

When Clint entered the dining room he gave the man seated at his table a quick once-over. He was apparently in his sixties, with a head of luxurious white hair, and a white mustache. His face was relatively unlined for a man his age, and his complexion pink. Seated, he appeared to be a fair-sized man. He appeared to be very uncomfortable sitting there by himself.

Clint's table was against the wall, and Wentworth had taken a chair with his left side against the wall, leaving the chair with its back-against the wall for Clint. Clint was sure that Highbinder had made certain that chair would remain vacant.

Wentworth's eyes were sweeping the room, and as he noticed Clint drawing closer and closer he gave all his attention to him.

As Clint reached the table, Wentworth said quickly, "Mr. Adams?"

"That's right," Clint said. He moved around and sat with his back to the wall. He put his hand against the pot of coffee that was on the table and was not satisfied with the heat he felt, so he didn't pour himself a cup. "You're Mr. Wentworth, Luke Short's friend?"

12

"That's right, Mr. Adams," Wentworth said. "I must say I'm not very happy about being forced to come down here to this—"

"Hold it, Mr. Wentworth," Clint said, holding up one hand, palm outward. "Nobody forced you to come here. You're here because you want to hire me."

"You could have come to my office—"

"No, Mr. Wentworth," Clint said coldly, "if you want to hire me, you come to *my* office."

"Which is where?"

Clint grinned tightly and said, "This is it."

He ignored Wentworth then as the waitress came to the table with his breakfast.

The waitress was a girl named Leona Gore, who had been working at the hotel the last time Clint was there. He had liked her then, and he had spent some exciting moments with her, but this trip something always seemed to be keeping him from getting reacquainted with her. During Clint's first week there—on this second visit—he had suggested to his friend Terence White that she be given a raise. Since then she waited on him every time he ate in the hotel.

She was a compactly built woman with hair that was too light to be called brown but too dark to be called blond. She was very pretty, with full lips, brown eyes, and heavy eyebrows. Clint knew that a lot of women these days plucked hairs from their eyebrows to shape them the way they wanted them, but Leona seemed content to leave her eyebrows alone. Clint liked her for that.

"Good morning, Clint," she said brightly. "Here's your breakfast."

"Thanks, Leona."

She put a plate of eggs, bacon, and potatoes down in front of him, and a basket of hot biscuits at his left elbow.

"I'll bring a fresh pot of coffee in a minute," she promised.

"Fine," Clint said.

"Would your friend like anything?"

"Mr. Wentworth?"

"Nothing, thank you."

"That's all, Leona."

"I'll be right back, then."

"Mr. Adams—" Wentworth said, but Clint raised his hand to cut him off.

"Wait," Clint said, and watched Leona walk from the room.

"Mr. Adams, please—"

"Do you want to get down to business, Mr. Wentworth, or do you still want to discuss who should have gone to whose office?"

Wentworth opened his mouth to answer, thought better of it, and took a deep breath before continuing.

"Let's talk business, then," he finally said.

"I hope you don't mind if I eat while we talk," Clint said, and proceeded to do so without waiting for a reply.

"Mr. Adams, I don't know how much Luke Short might have told you—"

"Why don't we just pretend he didn't tell me anything, and take it from there?"

"Very well."

At that moment Leona, true to her word, returned with a fresh pot of coffee. Smiling, she poured Clint a cup, and then poured Wentworth another cup.

"Thank you," Wentworth said.

"Sure," she said, and looking at Clint put the fresh pot down and said, "I'll just take this one out of the way."

"Thanks, Leona."

"Enjoy your breakfast, Clint."

Wentworth waited for her to leave before speaking.

"Mr. Adams, my son is twenty-six years old. A grown man, to be sure, but sometimes his judgment leaves something to be desired."

"Like with women?"

"Yes," Wentworth said, "especially when it comes to women."

"Are you married, Mr. Wentworth?"

"Yes, I am," Wentworth said, appearing surprised at the question.

"Is your present wife the mother of your son?"

"Well . . . no . . . I divorced Jack's mother several years ago."

"And this is your second marriage."

"No, my marriage to Jack's mother was my second—and longest. This is my third."

"And your wife, is she younger than you are?"

"Why, yes—"

"Considerably younger?"

"See here, what has this got to do with—"

"I'm trying to get a handle on the kind of life you and your son lead, Mr. Wentworth. Does Jack still live at home with you?"

"He does."

Clint waited a few moments, chewing a mouthful of food and then washing it down with a sip of coffee.

"All right, why don't you continue."

"In the past I've questioned the kind of girls he's gone out with, but he's never gotten serious about any of them—until now."

"Who is the girl?"

"Her name is Angela Hong," he said, making a face. "As you may guess from her name, she is Chinese."

"Is that your objection, Mr. Wentworth?"

Wentworth frowned and said, "What do you mean?"

"I think my question was very clear," Clint said. "Do you object to the girl because she is Chinese?"

"Well . . . that *is* part of it," he said.

"Good," Clint said. "At least you're honest about it."

"Why would I lie?"

"A lot of men lie for a lot of different reasons, Mr. Wentworth," Clint said. "I just like to know whether I'm dealing with one of those men."

"Well, you are not!" Wentworth said frostily.

"Good, that's good to know," Clint said. "Go on, please."

"Well, Jack is talking nonsense now about marrying this girl. She's from Chinatown, for God's sake, where they're all thieves. . . . Mr. Adams, I'd simply like you to prove that this Angela Hong is after Jack for his—for *my*—money."

"Does Jack have any money of his own?"

"Some."

"And is he a good-looking boy?" Clint winced as he heard himself referring to a twenty-six-year-old man as a "boy."

"He is fairly handsome, yes."

"Could it be possible that Angela Hong really loves him?"

"Well, of course it's a *possibility*. . . ." Wentworth said.

"Well, as long as you admit that, there's a possibility that I'll prove that she is *not* just after his—or your—money. How would you feel about that?"

Wentworth frowned.

"I don't suppose you would—"

"I will not fabricate evidence to the contrary, no."

"I didn't mean—"

"I know what you meant," Clint said. "In any case, I'll be making my report to you, since you'll be paying me, and you can do with it what you want."

"You won't be talking to Jack?"

"I don't see why I'd have to," Clint said.

"Then you won't be telling him what you find out."

"As I said, I'll be telling *you* because you're paying me. I would hope that you'd then tell him what I tell you, but that would be up to you."

"You'll take the job, then?"

"As long as you understand one thing."

"What is that?"

"I don't usually take on this kind of job," Clint said. "In fact, I hate this kind of job, so that means I'm going to soak you."

"Soak me?"

"I'm going to charge you a lot of money for this, Mr. Wentworth, probably more than I'm worth."

Wentworth seemed taken aback by Clint's frankness.

"I'm a wealthy man, Mr. Adams," he said finally. "Whatever fee you think is fair, I will pay."

"I just told you, Mr. Wentworth, my fee will *not* be fair. It will have to be enough to compensate me for doing something I hate. Do you understand that?"

"I understand."

"And you'll pay?"

"I'll pay."

"Fine, then," Clint said. "Do you know where Angela Hong lives?"

"I've written it down," the man said, and handed a piece of paper to Clint. Clint read it and saw that Angela Hong didn't live very far from Ross Alley. He'd be able to kill two birds with one stone by seeing her *and* Toy Lee on the same visit to Chinatown.

"I've written my home and business addresses on the back."

"Yes, I see that," Clint said. Wentworth lived on Nob Hill— no surprise—and his office was in San Francisco's financial district.

"All right," Clint said, putting the piece of paper in his shirt pocket, "I'll need twenty-five hundred dollars."

"Now?"

"Do you have that much on you?"

"Well, yes—"

"Then I'll need it now."

Wentworth hesitated, then took out his wallet and counted out two thousand five hundred dollars in one-hundred-dollar bills, laying them on the table one at a time. Clint took the money, lifted the basket of biscuits, and put the money underneath.

"You understand that this is not my total fee?"

"I understand."

Clint sighed. He had taken the job even though he had tried to get the man *not* to hire him. Wentworth was not to be denied.

"Well . . . I guess I'd better be going. . . ." Wentworth said, rising.

"One more thing, Mr. Wentworth."

"Yes?"

"Why did you ask Short about me?"

"I didn't."

"Was I recommended by someone?"

"No," Wentworth said.

"Well, how did you get on to me, Mr. Wentworth?"

"I live in San Francisco, Mr. Adams," Wentworth said, "I live *and* work here, and I have certain . . . contacts around the city. I've heard of you. You have a certain reputation."

Clint accepted his explanation without doubt. He knew he had a reputation. He didn't like it—and he didn't complain about it as much as he used to—but he knew it, and he knew the kind of people it attracted. Luckily, most of them usually had money.

"What business are you in, Mr. Wentworth?"

"I'm a banker."

"Not surprising," Clint said. "Good day, Mr. Wentworth. I'll be in touch."

"Good day."

As Wentworth left the dining room he passed Leona Gore, who was on her way to see if everything was all right with Clint.

THREE

With Wentworth's twenty-five hundred dollars in his wallet, Clint would rather have played poker than go poking around in Chinatown, but since the game did not start until that evening, he proceeded to Ross Alley.

A lot of *"lo-fan,"* which was what the Chinese called white people, were drawn to Chinatown. They didn't necessarily like Chinatown, but they were drawn to it by the women and the gambling and the opium.

Clint, on quite the other hand, liked Chinatown. For the most part it was a dismal, depressing place, both dirty and dangerous, but Clint somehow found it invigorating to be there. Every time he went to Chinatown, there was a better than even chance that he would not leave alive.

Hell, wasn't that enough to invigorate *any* man?

As usual, Ross Alley was dark. Day or night the alley was dark. As he walked through, the alley people—yellow *and* white—moved out of his way. They were all there looking for one of three things: gambling, opium, or whores.

To Clint's way of thinking the gambling was the least dangerous of the three. Drugs he had always found distasteful.

Anything that took control *away* from you was dangerous to Clint. As for the whores, some of them were very beautiful, but you never knew what kind of a disease you were going to take away with you—and it stayed with you after the post coital glow faded.

No, the gambling was the least distasteful. All it did was take your money, and they did that just as well in any hotel in Portsmouth Square.

Clint found the door to Toy Lee's establishment and knocked, knowing just what to expect. After a moment a small sliding panel opened and he saw a pair of almond-shaped, brown eyes that held not even a hint of intelligence.

"What?" Wang said.

"You know what, Wang," Clint said. "I don't come here except to see Toy Lee."

They went through the same song and dance every damn time. Clint had been there twice since arriving in San Francisco, for different reasons each time. Toy Lee knew his reputation, like Wentworth did, and Clint thought the old Chinaman was impressed with him—as an adversary.

"Open the fucking door, Wang."

Clint always said that and Wang always smiled. Clint *hated* when Wang smiled. That was when the abnormally big Chinaman was the most dangerous.

Clint decided to deviate from the script and make Wang stop smiling.

He out his Colt and pointed it at Wang's eyes through the panel. He didn't usually draw his gun unless he was going to use it, but he had to admit that this big Chinese man unnerved him.

"Open the damn door, Chinaman!"

He punctuated his order by cocking the hammer.

"You not shoot me," Wang's voice said. Wang was playing the ignorant Chinaman today. Clint knew the man could speak perfect English when he wanted to.

"If you don't open the door I most certainly will shoot you."

"I open door," Wang said, "I make you eat gun."

Clint would have been worried, but Wang had stopped smiling.

Clint heard the bolt thrown inside, and then the door swung open and Wang filled the doorway.

He was still not only the largest Chinaman he'd ever seen, but also the largest *man* of any color he'd ever seen.

Clint waggled the gun so Wang could see he was still holding it.

"You know, Wang, if you make me shoot you, Toy Lee's going to be very angry with you."

"And with you."

"I'll take that chance," Clint said. "I'd rather have Toy Lee angry at me than have you break me in half."

Wang smiled.

"Oh, yes, I know you *could* break me in half, Wang, but the point is, I have the gun, and before you could take one step I'd put a bullet in your knee. See, that way you wouldn't be able to walk, and you'd still be alive to explain to Toy Lee why you *made* me shoot you in the knee. Understand?"

"I understand," Wang said. Clint always wondered how Wang could blank his eyes like that, as if nothing were going on behind them.

"Can we go and see the man now?" Clint asked.

"One day, Clint," Wang said, dropping the sing song Chinaman accent, "one day."

"I know that, Wang," Clint said, "and I don't look forward to it."

"Wait here."

Clint put the gun away and said, "I'll wait right here, Wang."

The door closed and Wang disappeared, supposedly to get his orders from Toy Lee. Clint always suspected that when Wang closed the door he just stood behind it for a few minutes, making Clint wait, and didn't really go for orders at all. Clint thought that Wang had standing orders to let him see Toy Lee whenever he came here. Clint and Toy Lee had an understanding.

Clint and Wang had one, too, but it wasn't the same thing. Not at all.

Finally the door opened and Wang reappeared, filling the doorway again. Clint was a man who took great pride in his ability to handle himself in any kind of encounter. He was also a man who knew when he'd met his match. In Wang, he knew he had met his physical match. He might beat the man in a fight, but it would be on superior speed or smarts, certainly not on any physical superiority.

Still, it would be interesting.

"You may enter," Wang said, the words he always used.

Clint sighed, shook his head, and as he stepped past the big Chinaman said, "We really have to get a new act, Wang."

Clint waited for Wang to lock the door, then followed him down the familiar hall. At the end was a thick wooden door that Wang opened with a key. They entered, and Clint again waited for Wang to lock the door behind them. After that they went through a curtained doorway into the main gambling room.

As usual it was hard to see because of all the smoke, but after a moment Clint's eyes adjusted. He followed Wang through a sea of gamblers who refused to be distracted from their games long enough to look at him. The walk across this floor was always kind of dehumanizing.

They stopped at a door set in the back wall, and Wang knocked.

FOUR

"Come!" Toy Lee's voice called out, and Wang opened the door and allowed Clint to precede him.

Nobody knew exactly how old Toy Lee was. He could have been fifty, or a hundred, but however old he was, he ruled the gambling in Chinatown with an iron hand.

He was small and frail with wrinkled yellow skin and wispy white hair that seemed thinner every time Clint saw him.

He was wearing the same flowing robes he always wore, the kinds with flowing sleeves that made his arms look like twigs. The ashtray on the table had several crushed-out cigars in it. Toy Lee dispensed opium but never used it himself. He settled for regular tobacco.

"Clint," Toy Lee said, "my friend."

We all definitely need a new act, Clint thought.

"Hello, Lee."

"Tea?"

"No."

"Can I have Wang—"

"No."

Toy Lee looked at Wang and said, "You may go."

Clint knew that when Wang backed out of the room and closed the door, he stayed right on the other side.

"Some whiskey, perhaps," Lee said, still playing host. "Or a pipe?"

"Stuff your pipes, Lee. I wouldn't inhale that shit with your lungs."

"A wise man," Lee said, "I always said you were a wise man."

"Yeah," Clint said, "that's me, the fourth wise man."

"The fourth?" Lee asked. "Who are the other three?"

"You heathen," Clint said, "don't you know anything about Christmas?"

"I am Buddhist," Lee said, bowing. "We do not have Christmas."

"Must be a boring Christmas morning at your house," Clint said. He wondered then if Toy Lee *had* a house, or a family.

"What can I do for you, Clint?"

"Do you know a girl named Angela Hong?"

"Very well."

Clint was surprised—although he didn't know why he should be. He'd figured it a long shot that Lee would know some little Chinese gold digger, but then maybe Lee *did* know everyone and everything in Chinatown.

"How do you know her?"

"I know her family—or rather, I knew her family."

"What happened to them?"

"Her parents were stoned to death by angry miners in Shasta County when she was younger," Toy Lee said. "As you know, miners often employed Chinese, and then blamed them when their mines ran dry."

"I've heard. Does she have any family left?"

"A brother."

"Younger or older?"

"Older."

"How old are they?"

"Angela is twenty-two, I believe. Her brother, Jimmy, is twenty-seven, or -eight."

"What does he do?"

Toy Lee shrugged bony shoulders.

"What does a Chinese do in this country, my friend? He survives."

"I understand she's got herself a boyfriend," Clint said. "A *lo-fan*."

Lee's face betrayed nothing.

"I believe I've heard that."

"A rich white man—or the son of a rich white man."

"Ah . . ." Lee said.

"What do you mean, 'ah'?"

"I see why you are here."

"Why?"

"The rich man wants to know if the evil yellow woman is after his money."

"Not in so many words, but that's it."

Toy Lee frowned.

"Not your kind of job, I think."

"The man is *very* rich."

"Ah," Toy Lee said, "I see. Are you willing to pay for the information you seek?"

"You know I don't pay you, Lee," Clint said. "You talk to me because we're such great friends."

Toy Lee grinned, showing yellow teeth, and said, "I cannot tell you if Angela is after your employer's money or not."

"Could you find out?"

"I could, but I will not."

"You won't help me?"

"No."

"Lee, I'm crushed."

"If she is after his money, I applaud her ingenuity. If she is not after the money and truly loves this white man, then I feel sorry for her. If they marry, theirs will not be an easy life."

"Whose is?"

Toy Lee smiled and said, "Very true. You dispense philosophy like a true Chinese man, Clint."

"I'll take that as a compliment."

"It was meant as such."

"I'll need to poke around Chinatown, Lee. I won't have to watch my back, will I?"

Toy Lee took a moment or two to light up a fresh cigar, taking great care with the flame to get the cigar going just right.

Again Lee smiled.

"No more than usual, Clint."

"That's what I wanted to know, Lee," Clint said, ready to leave. He started for the door, then stopped and turned back to face the little man behind the desk.

"Lee, if you don't mind I'd much rather not go out the way I came in. It's depressing."

Toy Lee exhaled some smoke and watched it curl its way to the ceiling.

"Because you lose your money in high style," Lee said, studying the smoke, "you find those poor souls out there depressing?"

"No," Clint said, "I find them depressing because *they* lose."

"Ah," Lee said, "and you do not."

"Not usually, Lee," Clint said. "You should know that by now."

"Everyone loses sometime, Clint."

"Well," Clint said, moving toward the back door, "let's hope that in my case it's not sometime soon, huh, Lee?"

FIVE

After Clint had gone, Toy Lee mashed out his cigar, rose from behind his desk, and walked to the door. When he opened it he saw Wang standing right outside, with his massive arms folded across his chest like a wood Indian.

Wang looked down at Toy Lee but did not speak. He *would* not speak until he was spoken to.

Toy Lee looked over the room and saw that it was a busy night. Had it not been he would have sent Wang on the errand tonight, but as it stood, he would have to wait until the next morning.

There was also the possibility that the man he wanted to see was actually in the room, gambling, but he did not see him present.

"Wang."

"Yes, master."

"I have an errand for you to run in the morning."

"As you say, master."

"I want you to find a man for me and bring him here."

"Who, master?"

"I want you to find Jimmy Hong and bring him here."

"Yes, master."

"Wang."

"Yes?"

Toy Lee knew that Wang did not like Jimmy Hong. He thought the younger man disrespectful of the old ones, like Toy Lee, and did not approve.

He was right, though.

"Don't hurt him, Wang," Toy Lee said, "just bring him here. Understood?"

Wang shrugged his huge shoulders and said, "Yes, master."

At that moment Jimmy Hong was talking with his sister, Angela, in their one-room apartment not far from Ross Alley. There was a blanket strung across the center of the room, to divide Angela's sleeping area from Jimmy's. Jimmy remembered a time when he would try to take a peek at his younger sister as she was bathing, or readying herself for bed. He recalled when he was twenty and she was fourteen, and he had peeked in on her. Even then she had been beautiful, with smooth skin and round breasts, big nipples, and a nice furry patch between her legs. He felt guilty about peeking, but he did it nevertheless.

Jimmy Hong loved women and sometimes wished Angela *wasn't* his sister. He didn't feel guilty about that. Not anymore.

"So," he asked, "how are you and your *lo fan* lover doing?" he asked in perfect English. Long ago, after the death of their parents, Jimmy had decided that both he and his sister should learn to speak English as well as possible. He now spoke it almost without accent, while Angela still retained some of her accent. That was all right, though. He knew that men—especially white men—liked to hear the accent on the women—especially the pretty Chinese women.

"Get any money out of him yet?" Jimmy asked.

"I have told you, Jimmy," she said calmly, "I love him. I do not want his father's money."

"I'll bet his father would pay plenty for you to stay away from him."

"I am sure he would," she said, "but I do not intend to stay away."

"That's too bad, sis," he said. "We sure could use the money."

Angela did not look at her brother. She knew she would see that look of greed in his eyes and on his face. She thought the look made him ugly.

"I am going to sleep now, Jimmy."

"All right, sis," he said, and she went behind the blanket.

Jimmy lay on his bed for a few moments, wondering if he should try to get a peek at his sister now.

He bet she was really something to see naked.

Sometimes, late at night like this, Angela Hong thought about her parents. She thought about when they had all lived in China, and her father talked about the golden mountain, where even a Chinese family could go and become rich.

Her Uncle Soo had gone, and when he came back with more money than had ever been seen in their village, he convinced his brother—Angela's father—to take his family and return with him, to find his fortune.

On the ship, tragedy struck. A sailor tried to rape her mother, and when Uncle Soo stepped in, he was stabbed and killed. When Angela and Jimmy and their parents arrived in the United States, they were alone, with no one to guide them, as Uncle Soo was supposed to do.

Those early days were very hard. The four of them lived in one room, for which they paid dearly. Her father worked in a laundry, and her mother—she later found out—worked in a whorehouse. After a few years of that they left San Francisco with another Chinese family and headed for the Shasta Valley, where they mined for gold.

When the mines in Shasta dried up the miners had to blame somebody, so they picked on the Chinese, killing several of them by stoning—including Angela and Jimmy Hong's parents.

Angela and Jimmy traveled back to San Francisco with the surviving Chinese miners, and had been on their own ever since.

Over the past couple of years, though, Angela had felt even more alone than usual. She felt as if she and Jimmy were growing farther and farther apart as they got older. She didn't even know what he did to get the money he made, and she was afraid to guess.

She'd felt very alone until she'd met Jack Wentworth. He had been gambling in one of the parlors, and she had been being accosted by a *lo fan* on the street when Jack came out. He helped her, and walked her home, and then asked if he could see her again.

They had gone on from there. Since then she felt less alone, and he stopped gambling to please her. That was just two months ago.

Later she found out that his father was rich, and had made the mistake of telling Jimmy. Ever since then he was always asking her if her *lo fan* lover had given her any money.

Jack offered her money many times, but she had never taken it. Even if Jack *had* given her money, she wouldn't have told Jimmy.

She didn't know if she trusted her own brother anymore.

That thought always made her feel very alone all over again.

SIX

"Raise," Clint said, looking across the table at Dom Asher.

Asher was sitting pretty with three of a kind on the table. He needed a full house to beat Clint, however, because Clint had his heart flush.

Of course, Asher didn't know whether Clint had that fifth heart in the hole, and he'd have to pay to find out.

That is, unless he *had* the full house. Then it would be Clint who would pay.

That was why they called it gambling.

Clint decided not to track down Angela Hong immediately following his meeting with Toy Lee. He wanted to see what came of the meeting, first. It was possible that Toy Lee would talk to the girl, and that would be the end of it.

He doubted it, but it *was* a possibility.

Instead, he returned to the Silver Spur and took a long nap in preparation for the game that night.

Asher looked across the table at Clint, sighed, and said, "Call," pushing his money into the pot.

Clint just flipped over that fifth heart, and Asher folded his cards.

Luke Short gathered up the cards for the next deal, but somebody suggested a short break.

"Any objections?" Short asked.

There was none.

"A half an hour good enough?"

Everyone agreed it was fine. That was enough time for the players with rooms in the Alhambra to freshen up, and for others to get a drink from the bar, or try their luck at roulette.

Clint decided to go for a drink, and was standing at the bar when Luke Short walked in. He knew Short had seen him, so he raised his glass in greeting.

"Where's your shadow?" Clint asked.

"Who? Oh, Bat? I think he's busy tonight, maybe with a waitress."

The bartender, familiar with Short by this time, brought over a beer.

"I understand you saw Wentworth."

"We talked."

"Did you take the job?"

"I guess it would be up to him to tell you," Clint said, "seeing as how you're friends, and all."

"Not friends," Short said, "not really."

Short waited to see if Clint would ask any questions, but Clint was not notorious for his curiosity—not when it didn't directly affect him. The relationship of Short and Wentworth was something he didn't find himself wondering about.

"I had a debt to him is all," Short said.

"And now it's paid off?"

"Yes."

"That's fine."

"You don't mind?"

"Mind what?"

"That I used my, er, acquaintance with you to pay off an old debt."

"Why would I mind?" Clint said. "If he hired me, then I'm making money, right?"

"Right."

"So he's happy, I'm happy, and you're happy. Nothing wrong with that."

"I suppose not," Short said, sipping his beer. "Still, it bothered me some. I just wanted to . . . to let you know."

"I appreciate it."

Short studied Clint for a few moments and then said, "You're a strange one, Clint."

"Is that right?"

"Do you have a lot of friends?"

"Some."

"Anybody you'd trust to watch your back?"

"I'd trust you to watch my back," Clint said, "and I'd trust Bat."

"I'm flattered."

"Don't be," Clint said. "I simply know that you're both capable of covering me."

"Oh."

Clint grinned then and added, "And I count both of you among my not-so-many friends."

SEVEN

Toy Lee studied Jimmy Hong across his desk the next morning. He knew Jimmy was twenty-eight, but he could have passed for eighteen, especially when he smiled.

"What did you want to see me about, Toy Lee?" Jimmy asked.

Wang had shown Jimmy into the office and then left to take up his position at the front door. Even when there was no business being done—except upstairs, where the dens were—Wang stayed at his post at the front door. With Clint Adams, he stayed outside the office door, but Toy Lee was in no danger from Jimmy Hong.

"We must talk about your sister, Angela, Jimmy," Toy Lee said.

"About Angela?"

"Yes."

"What about her?"

Toy Lee's face was impassive, unreadable as he inclined his head and said, "Sit down, boy. . . ."

Angela Hong was worried.

Jack was supposed to have met her here, in an alley just at

the outer tip of Chinatown, and he wasn't here yet.

What could be keeping him?

The other thing that was bothering her was that Wang had come for Jimmy this morning, and that meant that Toy Lee wanted to see her brother.

What kind of trouble had he gotten himself into now?

It never occurred to her that Toy Lee and her brother might be talking about *her* at that very moment.

There were two other people talking about her that morning as well.

Samuel Wentworth was fuming, glaring at his son, Jack. He'd caught the boy just before the boy had gone out the door.

"Jack, you're going to see that girl!" he said accusingly.

"Papa, please," Jack said, "I don't want to get into this so early in the day."

"Why? Is there an ideal time to discuss how you're breaking your father's heart?"

"Excuse me, Papa," Jack said, "but if you *had* a heart you wouldn't be as successful in business as you are."

"That's a hell of a thing to say to your father," Linda Wentworth said.

She had come down the stairs from the second floor of the house without either man hearing her. Now they both looked at her.

At thirty-four Linda Wentworth was twenty-one years younger than her husband. Jack thought she was one of the most beautiful women he had ever seen, and wished they could be friends. The fact of the matter was, they didn't like each other very much. True, he had often felt some *sexual* tension between them, but even if he went to bed with her, he didn't think he'd like her very much.

She was tall, dark-haired, and full-bodied. All of Samuel Wentworth's wives had one thing in common: They were all full-bodied, large-bosomed women.

"I'm sorry, Linda," he said, trying to head off a full-fledged argument.

Linda came down the rest of the way and took hold of her husband's right arm possessively.

"Don't apologize to me," she said, "apologize to your father."

"Papa—"

"Never mind," Wentworth said, waving his hand. "Go to your Chinese . . . just go! Your relationship with this girl won't last very much longer, anyway."

Jack, whose hand had been on the doorknob this whole time, removed it. He turned and stared at his father. There was a hollow feeling in the pit of his stomach. He knew the methods his father used in his business. Would he dare use them now?

"What do you mean?" he demanded. "What have you done, Papa?"

"Never mind—"

"What are you *going* to do?"

"Never mind," Wentworth said forcefully. "I don't want to discuss it any further. Dear," he said to his wife, "let's see if breakfast is ready."

As Wentworth turned away, Jack wanted desperately to pursue the matter further, but he knew his father would not budge. He also knew that he was not strong enough to *make* him budge. Also, he was late in meeting Angela now, and he knew she'd worry—just as he worried about her in Chinatown. He wanted to get her out of there as soon as possible, but she wouldn't leave her brother.

Two men were keeping her from marrying him: his father and her brother.

If they could just convince both of them that this thing between them was *real,* that it would last. If they could just convince them to leave them alone!

He shook his head, grasped the doorknob tightly, and left.

EIGHT

Clint woke that morning feeling good. The first two nights had not gone well for him in the game, but last night had gone *very* well. Maybe it was because he'd been playing with the money he'd gotten from Wentworth.

The only person who had done better than he last night had been Masterson. Clint knew that Masterson was a better poker player than he was, but last night his luck had almost matched that of Bat Masterson.

He went downstairs and let Leona Gore bring him breakfast.

"I'll bring the coffee right away, Clint," she said, and hurried away.

As he began eating, he saw Terence White enter the dining room.

White saw Clint and started across the room. Terence was in his late thirties. His slick, black hair came to a widow's peak, and his goatee combined with that to give him a satanic look. It wasn't accidental. Without the goatee White had a weak chin. He preferred looking satanic. He did better with women. As usual, he was immaculately dressed without looking foppish.

"What are you doing here?" Clint asked.

"Can't I sample the food in my own dining room once in a while?" White said, taking the chair to Clint's left.

"Once in a *great* while," Clint said. "To what do I owe this pleasure?"

Leona had seen White enter and hurried over to take his order. She brought him an empty coffee cup.

"Good morning, Mr. White."

"Good morning, Leona," White said, eyeing her appreciatively. "Just bring me what Clint's having."

"Right away, sir."

"And don't call me 'sir,' all right?" he said, smiling.

"Yes, si—I mean, yes."

He watched her walk to the kitchen, then turned his head and looked at Clint.

"Have you made her yours yet?"

"What?"

"Do you think I don't have eyes?"

"She's a nice kid."

"Sure."

"Drop it."

White said "sure" again, in a different tone of voice.

White poured himself a cup of coffee and drank some of the scalding liquid without reacting to the heat.

"You must have wooden lips," Clint said.

"I like things hot," White said, putting down his cup. "My coffee, my food, my women . . . the only thing I don't like hot is somebody's breath down my neck."

"What's that mean?"

"I saw Samuel Wentworth leaving here yesterday," White said. "Was he here to see you, or me?"

"Me. Why?"

"Don't you know who he is?"

"I don't read the financial page, Terry."

"He's on the financial page, the society page—shit, he's all over the newspaper."

"So why does him being here worry you?"

"Because when he walks into a hotel like this one—bigger ones, even—they usually end up getting swallowed up."

"Swallowed up?"

"Bought."

"He buys hotels?" Clint asked. "He told me he was in banking."

"He is. He finances large purchases—of hotels, banks, ranches. If it's a big deal, he's usually the man who handles it."

"Are you looking to sell?" Clint asked.

"Hell, no—but sometimes he doesn't wait for somebody to offer, if you know what I mean."

"He *takes* them?"

"He makes an offer that can't be turned down—like half what the property is worth . . . and your life."

"Well, he wasn't here to buy the hotel, or take it," Clint said. "He was here to hire me."

"Well, that's a relief," White said. "I thought I was going to have to watch you and him—and his people—go head to head."

"Where would your money be on that one?"

"Ask me something else," White said. "You and he don't work in the same circles. It might be an interesting match at that. What did he hire you for . . . if I may be so bold as to ask?"

"His son's running around with a gold digger, or so he thinks."

"What's he want you to do, give her a beating and warn her off?"

"Just prove she's after the old man's money."

"And if she isn't?"

"He's going to be real disappointed."

Leona came with White's breakfast and asked Clint if

she could get him anything else.

"I'm fine, Lee."

"Let me know if you need me, Clint."

She walked away, and White looked at his friend.

"Don't say it," Clint warned him.

NINE

Jimmy Hong was confused.

Why, he wondered, would Toy Lee be worried about Angela's relationship with Jack Wentworth? Why would the old man instruct him—*order* him—to see that his sister did not continue this relationship?

The only possible answer he could see was that Toy Lee did business with Jack Wentworth's rich father—whoever and whatever he was.

It was time Jimmy Hong found out just who his sister was really dallying with.

"Jack" was all he had ever heard from Angela. The "Wentworth" had come from Toy Lee, and Jimmy had made sure that the old man—whom he had first met when he was ten—did not realize that he had not known "Jack's" last name until that moment.

Jimmy Hong had some contacts of his own in areas of San Francisco other than Chinatown.

Today he was going to put them to good use.

Samuel Wentworth was preoccupied all morning at his office, and it was very evident to his assistant, an ambitious young man named Robert Stock.

"Still having those problems at home, Mr. Wentworth?" Stock asked.

"Huh?" Wentworth said. "What was that, Bob?"

"The problems at home," Bob Stock said solicitously. "They're still bothering you."

"Oh," Wentworth said, leaning back in his chair. "It's that evident, is it?"

"Yes, sir."

"I guess I have been a little preoccupied this morning."

"That's all right, sir."

"Luckily I've got you to make sure my business doesn't fall down around my ears."

Stock straightened and said, "I do my best, sir."

Bob Stock was his son's age, and more and more Wentworth found himself wishing that Jack was more like Stock.

"If you'll allow me to say so, sir . . ." Stock said.

"What is it, Bob?"

"Well, I have some friends, sir," Stock said. "If you'd care to let me take care of your problem—"

"What do you know of my problem?" Wentworth asked quickly.

"I'm sorry, sir, but it's not exactly a secret that Jack is seeing a . . . a Chinese girl."

"No," Wentworth said, relaxing somewhat, "I don't suppose that it is."

"I could handle it for you, sir."

"That's all right, Bob," Wentworth said. "I've already got someone handling it for me."

Stock was taken aback. This was his big chance, and he didn't want to blow it. If he could handle this for the old man, his future would be assured.

"Sir?"

"I hired someone."

"An outsider?"

"Yes," Wentworth said, "yes, an outsider. His name is Clint

Adams. He has a . . . certain reputation."

"Clint Adams," Stock said, nodding. "I've heard of him, sir. This doesn't strike me as his usual sort of business."

"It's not," Wentworth said, "but he was willing to take it on for . . . for some *extra* consideration."

"Money?"

"And lots of it. As he said, he was going to *soak* me for doing a job he hated, but if he gets it done, it will be worth it."

Stock bit his lip. Stupid old man!

"Sir, if you change your mind," he said after a few moments, "if Adams doesn't get the job done, please consider what I've said."

"Hmm? Oh, of course, Bob, of course. Now," Wentworth said, sitting forward, "tell me about this theater we're supposed to be buying. . . ."

TEN

Clint went to Chinatown that day. He went to the address he had for Angela and Jimmy Hong, but there was no one at home. He stood with his back against the door for a moment, trying to decide whether to wait there for the girl or go looking for her. Only where would he look?

He was the center of attention on the street. He was the only *lo fan,* plus he was six feet tall, much taller than any of the Chinese who were passing by. Some of them knew who he was; others just knew he was a dangerous-looking *lo fan* they wanted no part of.

He finally decided to take a turn around Chinatown and see what he could find, after which he'd return here and try again.

He pushed away from the door just as the shot was fired. A bullet struck the door, sending wood chips into his eyes. Blindly he threw himself to the ground, rubbing at his eyes with one hand and pulling his gun with the other.

He rolled in the dirt and came up against the wall on the opposite side of the street. As he came up to one knee he was still pawing at his eyes, unable to see clearly. He could still hear, though, and when he heard the second shot, he threw himself to the ground again. He kicked up dust, which also got into his eyes, and now he was effectively blind—helpless!

He had his gun in his hand but couldn't see to fire it. Suddenly a hand closed over his forearm.

"What—" he said, yanking it away.

"Come with me!" a voice hissed urgently.

"Who—"

"Unless you'd rather die?"

The voice was a woman's, and when he gave her his arm again, her grip was strong. She pulled him, and he allowed himself to be led. She was holding his free arm while he still held his gun, and his eyes were tearing. He considered pulling away from her to rub them, but maybe the tears would wash the dust and wood chips out.

There were two more shots, and one came so close he felt it go by his face.

"Faster!" the woman shouted, and pulled on his arm.

She ran with him in tow until they were out of range, then found an alley and pulled him into it.

"Get down," she said, and he hunkered down. She squatted next to him, and he felt her touching his eyes with something.

"It's only a cloth," she said. "Let me see if I can help."

Her touch was very gentle now as she swabbed out his eyes with the cloth, using his own tears to clean them. Gradually his eyesight came back, and he found himself looking into the face of an Oriental woman. She was frowning, and the tip of her tongue was protruding from one corner of her mouth. She could have been eighteen or thirty-eight at that moment, but he wasn't seeing clearly enough yet to make an accurate guess.

"What's your name?" she asked.

"Clint."

She stopped cleaning his eyes for a moment, then started again.

"Well," she said, "I *was* going to ask who would want to kill you, but I guess I don't have to now."

"You speak very good English," he said.

"Thank you. It was not without a lot of effort that I learned. Many of my people have started to try to learn to speak English well. I think they—we—feel it will help us be accepted more."

"It'll take more than that."

She laughed softly, and he felt her breath on his face as she leaned closer to examine his eyes.

"I know that."

She continued to clean his eyes, and after a few moments stopped and said, "Well, they look fairly clean. A little red-rimmed, but clean. Can you see?"

He blinked several times, and her face came into focus. Closer to eighteen, definitely, but no child. Probably twenty-five or so, and pretty except for a slightly flattened nose.

"Yes, thank you," he said.

"Maybe you'd better holster your gun now."

He realized he was still holding the weapon in his hand, and he put it away.

"We can stand up if you like," she said, and they did. She was much shorter than he, almost a foot. Her very black hair, cut short and parted in the center, framed her face.

"I'd like to thank you," he said. "You probably saved my life at great risk to your own."

"I couldn't just stand there and watch them shoot you," she said. "You couldn't see, and you were helpless."

" 'Them,' " he said.

"What?"

"You said 'them,' " he said. "Did you see who was doing the shooting?"

"Not exactly."

"But there were more than one?"

She nodded her head.

"I saw just one, on the roof across the street."

That explained why, after he had moved to the other side, they still had a clear shot at him.

"Have you ever seen him before?" he asked.

She smiled and said, "*Lo fan,* you all look alike. If I have seen him before, I do not remember."

"Would you know him again if you saw him?"

"I don't think—" she began, then stopped and frowned, her tongue tip popping out again in the corner of her mouth. "I might recognize him. He had a very brown face—"

"A black man?"

"No," she said, shaking her head, "but a very brown face, and a nose like a hawk."

The description didn't ring any bells with Clint, but it might with someone else.

"What's your name?" he asked.

"My Chinese name or my American name?"

"One that I can pronounce."

"You may call me Jenny, then."

"Well, thank you, Jenny. I'd like to repay you in some way."

"You may, someday," she said.

"Maybe I can . . ." he said, putting his hand in his pocket.

"I am not a beggar," she said. "In fact, I was on my way to work when I stopped to help you. I hope I still have a job when I get there."

"Would you like me to come along—"

"That won't be necessary. Actually, I work for my uncle in his laundry. He won't fire me for being late—unless he discovers why." She smiled sheepishly at him and added, "He doesn't like *lo fan*."

"He probably has good reason not to," he said. "I'd like to do something—"

"Send me your laundry," she said, and, with a wave, bounded away from him.

"Wait—" he called out, but she was gone. He wanted to ask her if she knew Angela Hong, but it was too late.

He thought about going back to Angela Hong's residence, but his eyes were hurting and starting to tear again. He decided to see a doctor first.

He'd had a taste of being blind, and he didn't like it. He wanted to make *sure* his eyes were all right.

ELEVEN

"What the hell happened to you?" Terence White asked as Clint entered the hotel lobby.

"Let's go to the office," Clint said.

"All right."

They went through a curtained doorway behind the desk, the desk clerk staring at Clint as he went by. The clerk was new. They never seemed to be able to hold on to their desk clerks. The bellboys—Highbinder and four others—had been with them for some time, but the turnover of clerks was tremendous. White said it was because Clint scared them.

"I hardly ever talk to them," Clint had replied.

"I know. Highbinder talks to them for you. I don't know what he tells them, but they all become scared of you and eventually leave."

"That's crazy."

Later, Highbinder told him that White was correct.

"We've had three new clerks since you've been here, and every one of them has asked me about you."

"And what do you tell them?"

"Nothing," Highbinder said, and Clint believed him, "but

that just makes them more curious, and when their curiosity isn't satisfied, it turns to fear."

Clint still thought it was crazy, but he continued to ignore the desk clerks, and they continued to stare at him whenever he went by.

Now they walked down a hallway to a heavy oak door. White opened it with a key, and they went inside.

The office was plushly furnished to White's taste. He had done almost the entire office in leather. Even the desk had leather trim.

White sat behind the desk in his huge leather chair, and Clint took the other chair, facing the desk. It was also leather, but not as stuffed as White's chair.

"Want to tell me what happened now?"

Clint told him, and White sat forward and studied Clint's eyes.

"Are you all right?"

"I saw your doctor," Clint said. There was a doctor's office two blocks away. The doctor's name was Carl Boyer, and White used him whenever someone was sick or injured in the hotel.

"He said no damage had been done to the eyes, but he cleaned them out and said I should wash them out with warm water every so often for the next two days."

"How do they feel?"

"Like there's a pound of dirt in each of them," Clint said. "He said they'd feel that way for a few days."

"What about the shooter?"

"I didn't see him, but Jenny did."

"The Chinese gal?"

Clint nodded.

"Can she identify him?"

"Maybe one of them," Clint said, and described the man. "It didn't bring anybody to mind for me. What about you?"

"Dark skin, big nose—"

"Hawk nose."

"Right, so it's probably a big nose with a hook in it or

something like that at the end."

"Right."

"Distinctive," White said, "but it doesn't ring any bells for me, either."

"See what you can find out from your contacts," Clint said. "They must have been pros. They had both sides of the street covered."

"But they missed."

"I moved pretty fast," Clint said, not modest, not bragging, "and so did the girl."

"I'll see what I can find out."

Before White had gone into the hotel business he had been an expert con man. He had many contacts on the "other" side of the law.

Clint stood up and rubbed his eyes with his thumb and forefinger.

"Don't do that," White said.

"That's what the doc said," Clint admitted, dropping his hand. "He also told me to rest them, so I'm going to my room."

"Hey," White said, stopping Clint at the door.

"What?"

"This . . . incident really got to you, didn't it?" White was looking at his friend with concern.

Clint dropped his hand from the doorknob and faced his friend.

"Terry, for a few moments—and that's all it was—I was totally blind. Believe me, it wasn't a very good feeling. Even when the girl came, I had to depend on someone else for my survival for the first time in my life. *That* wasn't a very good feeling, either."

"No, I guess it wouldn't be."

Clint grabbed the doorknob again and said, "I'll be in my room for a few hours."

"Need Highbinder to wake you?"

"I don't think so," Clint said. "If you don't see me in three hours, though, send him up."

"All right. Want some food in your room?"

"Yeah, why not? Send it up in a few hours. That'll work as well as a wake-up."

"You got it," White said, then grinned and added, "Maybe I'll have Leona bring it up. She could run your eyes for you."

"You're a dirty old man, Terence White," Clint said, and left.

He took the hallway the opposite way from the way they had come and took the back stairs to his floor, the second. The hotel had three floors, but he didn't want to be that high up. They had knocked down the wall between two rooms to make one large one for him, and White had a similar room on the third floor.

Clint approached his room, feeling tired and angry. Somebody had sent two killers after him, and it wasn't bad enough that they'd tried to kill him, they had also made him feel helpless.

Somebody was going to pay for that.

He was about to open the door when he stopped short. From beneath the door he thought he had detected movement, maybe a shadow.

Someone was in the room.

He removed his Colt from his holster, keyed the door, and opened it.

TWELVE

It was a woman, and she was sitting in his chair.

"You don't need that gun," she said.

"That's what you say."

From the small table she picked up her purse and threw it to him. He caught it, hefted it, and tossed it back to her.

"Want to see my legs now?" she asked.

"Sure."

She didn't hesitate. She lifted her skirt high enough for him to see the whites of her thighs. She had long legs, with soft, full thighs and shapely calves. No guns.

He holstered his gun and she let her skirt drop—to the floor! Her top followed after that, and then she was naked. This time she was lady and slut at the same time, and he remembered her name. At least when he'd met her at the Alhambra she'd *said* her name was Linda. He didn't have any reason to doubt her.

She came to him and undressed him, and he automatically palmed her breasts, without even thinking. She gasped, bit her lip, and let her head loll back on her neck. He leaned over and pressed his lips to her neck, then down to her breasts and those incredibly responsive nipples. . . .

• • •

She was thirty-four, with dark hair, a long, smooth neck, a full mouth that was slightly crooked, wide-set brown eyes, and carefully cared-for eyebrows.

She was a classy, sexy lady, and she knew it. He lay in bed and watched her dress. It was a special pleasure of his, watching women dress. He enjoyed it almost as much as watching them *un*dress.

"My name is Linda," she said. "Linda Wentworth."

"Samuel's wife?" he asked, stunned.

She nodded.

"Which one?"

She smiled and said, "The current one."

He got out of bed and grabbed for his clothes. The first time he'd slept with her she had just been a woman he'd met in a gambling hall. Now she was the wife of the man he worked for.

Coincidence!

God, how he hated that word.

"How did you get in here?"

"My husband took me away from a life of crime," she said frankly. "I know how to open doors without a key. He caught me in his office one night and didn't call the police."

"Sounds like a story with a happy ending, Mrs. Wentworth," he said.

"Almost," she said.

"What about—"

She knew what he was going to ask, and answered it before he was finished.

"My husband is older than I am. You know that. Sometimes I just . . . need to be with someone younger, someone who can . . . satisfy my needs."

It was obvious that she enjoyed sex very much. Why would a woman like that marry a man who *couldn't* satisfy her? The answer to that was easy money.

She was an incredibly sexy lady. He wondered how Jack Wentworth could live in the same house with her.

"To what do I owe the pleasure of this intrusion, Mrs. Wentworth?"

"I understand my husband hired you."

He reached for his eyes to rub them, caught himself, and lowered his hand.

"Did he?"

"Didn't he?"

He stared at her and said, "You're telling it, Mrs. Wentworth."

"Well, since you knew who my husband was—and knew enough to ask *which* wife I was—I assume he was here to hire you."

"Your deductions are sound, Mrs. Wentworth, but just because he was here to hire me doesn't mean that he did."

"Well . . . he did."

"Did he tell you that?"

"Not in so many words."

"How many words *did* he use?"

"I heard it from . . . another source."

"Well, that's fine, Mrs. Wentworth. If you want to confirm it, why don't you ask your husband?"

"He wouldn't tell me," she said. "He doesn't discuss his business with me."

"I see."

Did she think that he had been hired by her husband in some business capacity? He wondered what—or who—her source was.

"In any case, Mrs. Wentworth," Clint said, "what can I do for you?"

"*I* would like to hire you, Mr. Adams."

"To do what, Mrs. Wentworth?"

"To protect my husband."

"Against what?"

"Against . . . anything."

"You have to be more specific than that, Mrs. Wentworth."

"Stop calling me that," she said. "Just a little while ago you were calling me Linda."

"That's before I knew who you were, Mrs. Wentworth."

She frowned, and answered the question he had asked.

"Against anyone who might try to do him harm."

"Is there someone who'd like to do him harm?"

"My husband is a very successful man, Mr. Adams," she said. "Successful men make a lot of enemies, but in this case I'm not thinking about *those* kind of enemies."

Clint's eyes were hurting and he wanted to go to sleep. As sexy as this lady was, he wanted her to leave.

"Mrs. Wentworth, I'm afraid we're not getting anywhere here, but in any case, I wouldn't be available for you to hire."

"Why not?" she asked, getting her classy back up.

"I'm already working," he said. "I only take one job at a time."

"I see. Well, Mr. Adams, the truth is, the two jobs may be related."

"In what way?"

"My stepson is seeing a Chinese girl, Mr. Adams. I'm sure that's what my husband hired you . . . about."

About, Clint thought. That meant that although she knew he'd been *hired,* she didn't know exactly *what* he had been hired to do.

"So?"

"I understand she has a brother, and I'm sure he has other heathen friends. I wouldn't want anything to . . . happen to my husband as a . . . a result of Jack's ill-advised . . . liaison."

Jesus, he thought.

"Did you talk like that when you were rifling rooms for a living, Mrs. Wentworth?"

She didn't take offense.

"As a matter of fact, no. It's something I cultivated after marrying my husband. Why, don't I carry it off well enough?"

"You carry it off very well, Mrs. Wentworth. I'd be willing to bet that you do whatever you want to do, and do it well."

"Why, thank you, Mr. Adams."

"But I have to ask you to leave now, Mrs. Wentworth. You're keeping me from my nap."

"A nap?" she said. "In the middle of the day?"

"We're all getting on in years, Mrs. Wentworth."

Out of everything he'd said to her over the past fifteen minutes, *that* seemed to insult her.

"Of course, I didn't mean you," he said. "You've got wonderful legs for a woman . . . what, twenty-eight or -nine?"

"Close," she said, standing up. "I'm thirty-four."

He was surprised at her admission. She struck him as being vain.

She walked to the door and then turned to face him with it at her back.

"I don't suppose you'd tell me exactly what my husband hired you to do, Mr. Adams?"

"You suppose—or don't suppose—correctly, ma'am."

She opened the door and left, leaving behind a scent that was going to make it hard for him to fall asleep.

He gave it a try, anyway.

THIRTEEN

He woke even before the knock on the door came, but just barely. He could still smell Linda Wentworth in the room.

He rose, wearing only shorts, and was in the act of opening the door before he recalled that Terence White had said he might send Leona up with the food. As he swung the door open he was relieved to see Sam Highbinder holding a covered tray of food.

"Come in, Sam," he said, backing away and letting go of the door.

Highbinder entered and looked around for someplace to put the tray.

"You need another table up here," he said.

"I don't eat here very often," Clint said. He was bending over a basin of water, bathing his face and his eyes. He'd forgotten about them when he first woke, but now felt the grittiness again. It wasn't the dust, dirt, and wood so much as it was the constant rubbing he'd done. In trying to clear them he had done more damage than the actual foreign matter that had entered his eyes—or so Doc Boyer had told him.

He turned and saw Highbinder making room on the small

table by his armchair and balancing the tray there.

"I don't know if it will stay—" Highbinder said.

"Don't worry about it," Clint said, patting his face and eyes dry with a towel.

"I'll pick up the tray later."

"Fine. I'll take care of you later."

Highbinder knew that Clint took care of him very well indeed, and was satisfied with the promise. He was at the door when he stopped, turned, and looked around. Clint knew that he, too, had picked up that peculiar scent that Linda Wentworth had left behind.

The scent of sex.

"Something wrong?" Clint asked.

"No, it's just . . ." Highbinder said, shrugging. "If I didn't know better I'd say . . . but I don't see . . . ah, never mind. I'll see you later, Clint."

Clint didn't say anything, and after Highbinder left he lifted the top off the tray. Maybe the smell of the food would over-power the scent of Linda Wentworth.

And then again, maybe not.

After Clint finished eating, he left his room and went for a walk. He was testing his eyes, making sure they'd stand up to the daylight and the open air. After a short walk he was satisfied that his eyes weren't going to fall out, so he changed direction and went into the saloon that was part of the hotel. He used the separate entrance, but there was another from the dining room as well.

He went to the bar, and the bartender, an ex-boxer named Willie, came over. The man's ears were mashed, and there was so much scar tissue over his eyes that he no longer had eyebrows. His nose had been broken more times than anyone could count. He was about fifty, and his arms and fists were still as hard as they'd been when he was in his prime. His belly protruded now, but even that was hard.

"What can I get you, Clint?"

"A beer, Willie."

"Comin' up."

When Willie brought the beer, Clint drank half of it and set the mug down on the bar.

"Trouble with your eyes?" Willie asked.

"Got some dirt in them."

Willie peered closely at Clint's eyes, and the latter picked up his mug and turned away.

"Must have been a lot of dirt," Willie said.

"Willie," Clint asked, "you have any idea what it's like to be blind?"

"Sure."

"You do?" Clint asked, surprised.

"Ten years ago I was in a fight," Willie said, leaning his massive forearms on the bar. "We was in the twenty-first round and the other guy cut me open, here." Willie pointed to a deep scar on his forehead. "Well, I tell you, the blood poured into my eyes and I just couldn't see. I was totally blind."

"What did you do?"

"I panicked and started swinging as hard as I could."

"And?"

Willie stood up and smiled and said, "I hit that referee so hard he was out for hours."

"And the other guy?"

Willie shook his head and said, "He did the same thing to me. I never saw the punch coming."

Clint finished the beer and put the mug down.

"Willie, thanks for the beer and the story."

"I got plenty of both."

That much was true. It made the Silver Spur Saloon one of the more popular drinking establishments off of Portsmouth Square.

As Clint was leaving, Willie called out, "Watch out for that dirt, Clint!"

Clint waved a hand behind him. When he found the two shooters, he was going to do worse to them than Willie had done to the referee in that fight.

A hell of a lot worse.

FOURTEEN

Clint knew he had to give Terence at least twenty-four hours to come up with information—if any—on the shooter's description he had gotten from Jenny. All he could do that evening was go to the Alhambra and play poker.

He played, but he played badly.

There were no general rest periods for the players now, but Clint and Luke Short managed to be in the saloon together at 3:00 A.M., drinking beer.

It struck Clint odd that Short seemed to be trying to keep tabs on the job Clint was doing for Samuel Wentworth. Maybe, since Short seemed intent on doing so, Clint could get some information out of him.

"Luke, what do you know about Mrs. Wentworth?" Clint asked.

"Which one?"

"The current one."

"Linda?"

"Yes."

"Not much," Short said. "She came along while I was out of touch with Samuel. The last time I saw him he was still married to Teresa—that's Jack's mother."

"So you don't know Linda well?"

"I don't know her at all, and I don't want to."

"Why not?"

"I don't have to know her to know she's dangerous, that one."

"How?"

"How is a woman dangerous? She *invites*—" Short started, then stopped.

"Attractive?"

Short rolled his eyes and said, "Very."

"What about Jack?"

"What about him?"

"What kind of man is he?"

"I know what kind of *kid* he was," Short said, "but I don't know much about what kind of *man* he is."

"What do you know?"

"What do you mean?"

"For somebody who's supposed to be a good friend of this man—"

"I never said we were good friends," Short said. "I said I *owed* him something, and this was my way of paying him off."

Off, Clint thought. Not paying him *back*, but paying him *off*.

"All right, Luke," Clint said, putting his beer mug down. "In the future, since you haven't anything to add, I'd appreciate it if you wouldn't pump me any."

"Pump you—"

"You know what I mean."

The two men stared at each other for a few moments, and then Short put his mug down.

"I'm going back upstairs. You coming?"

"No, I'm calling it quits for the night. I'll see you tomorrow."

After Short left, Clint had another beer. He wasn't able to

concentrate in the game because he was thinking about other things.

Linda Wentworth. Why had she really come to his room and, among other things, shown him her legs and made his dick tingle?

Jenny . . . whatever. He hadn't even gotten the girl's last name, and she'd saved his life. What had she been doing there at the time? Just passing by on her way to work, as she claimed?

And he was thinking about two men on rooftops with rifles, firing at him. Pros, and yet they had missed. *Had* he and Jenny been that fast, or were they supposed to miss?

Had he been warned? Was that it?

Warned about what?

To stay away from Angela Hong?

Who'd have reason to warn him off of her?

Her brother?

Her boyfriend?

It had to be the boyfriend. Two pros wouldn't work for a Chinaman, and Jimmy Hong wouldn't have the money to hire them even if they *would* have worked for him.

Maybe it was time for Clint to have another talk with his client, in the morning.

FIFTEEN

"Can I help you?"

Clint looked down at the man seated behind the desk. He'd been told that Mr. Stock was Mr. Wentworth's personal assistant—whatever that meant.

The man he was looking at was in his midtwenties, probably the same age as Wentworth's son.

"I'm here to see Mr. Wentworth."

"Do you have an appointment?"

"No."

"Then I'm afraid he can't see you," the man said in a tone of dismissal that made Clint's teeth grate.

"Look, this is a personal matter," Clint said. "He'll want to see me."

"I don't think . . ." the man started, then stopped and looked at Clint with renewed interest. "You're Clint, aren't you?"

"That's right."

The man continued to study him with interest.

"Will you tell him I'm here?"

"Is this about his son?"

"Like I said," Clint said, "it's a personal matter."

"Sure," the man said, pushing back his chair. "I'll tell him you're here. Wait here."

"I'm not going anywhere."

The man got up and went through a doorway. Clint stood right where he was until the man returned. He came back through the doorway and left the door open.

"He'll see you now."

"Thanks."

Clint moved toward the doorway, and the man stepped aside to let him through.

"What's your name?" Clint asked.

"Stock," the man said. "Robert Stock."

"What exactly does a personal assistant do?" Clint asked.

The question seemed to throw Stock, and Clint moved into the room and closed the door without waiting for an answer.

"Mr. Adams," Wentworth said from behind his desk. He was standing, looking uncomfortable for some reason. "I didn't expect—"

"Something's come up."

"What?"

Clint approached the desk.

"How many people have you told about hiring me?"

"Uh . . . specifically—"

"In any context."

"Well—"

"Let me help you," Clint said, ticking them off on his fingers. "Your wife?"

"Well—"

"Your son?"

"I didn't mention . . . your name—"

"Your *personal assistant* out there?"

"I didn't—"

"Mention my name?"

"Well . . . perhaps I did—"

"To him, or to your son?"

"To Bob," Wentworth said, "I think I may have mentioned your name to Bob, but not to my son."

"And your wife?"

"I may have mentioned your name, but not what I hired you to do."

"I have to tell you, Mr. Wentworth," Clint said, "none of this sits very well with me."

"I'm sorry, I didn't mean—"

"Somebody took a shot at me yesterday."

"What?"

"In fact," Clint went on, "*two* somebodies took several shots at me."

"My God, were you hurt? I—"

"I'm fine, just fine, but I'm not a happy man. Somebody doesn't want me looking for Angela Hong in Chinatown."

"I don't understand," Wentworth said. "Who would do such a—"

"That's what I wanted to find out from you," Clint said. He leaned forward, resting his palms on the man's desk, and his weight on his palms. "Who else did you tell, Mr. Wentworth?"

"No one, I—"

"A lawyer, a friend . . . a lover?"

Wentworth stood straight up.

"I beg your pardon. I have no . . . no one other than my wife."

"That's nice, Mr. Wentworth, that's real nice. I'd pat you on the back except somebody tried to kill me yesterday and I'd like to know who."

Wentworth slumped again and said, "I tell you I don't know."

"Well," Clint said, standing up straight, "do me a favor and think about it."

"You mean . . . you'll continue to work for me?"

"Only because I want to know who shot at me," Clint said.

"I'm terribly sorry, Mr. Adams," Wentworth said. "I had no idea—"

"Yeah, neither did I."

"Excuse me, but couldn't the attempt on your life be . . . unrelated to the work you are doing for me?"

"It could," Clint admitted.

"I mean, in your line of work—"

"I'm considering that possibility, Mr. Wentworth," Clint said, cutting the man off, "but the fact remains it happened only two days after you hired me."

"Yes, I realize—"

"And please," Clint added, "don't mention my name to anyone else."

"No, of course not."

"Tell me about your assistant out there, Stock."

"What do you want to know?"

"What kind of a man is he?"

"He's a fine boy—man. He's a hard, loyal worker—"

"What kind of a *man* is he, Mr. Wentworth?"

"Well, I don't know anything about his life outside this office, if that's what you're asking."

"That's what I'm asking."

"I'm sorry—"

"So am I, Mr. Wentworth," Clint said, moving toward the door. "I'll be in touch."

"Please . . ." Wentworth said, but Clint was out the door and didn't hear what would have come next.

In the other room Clint stopped and looked down at Robert Stock.

"Yes?" Stock asked, meeting his gaze.

"Thank you," Clint said.

"Oh, you're welcome. . . ."

Clint left without a backward glance. He was very curious about the man, and would have to do something to satisfy his curiosity.

SIXTEEN

Clint went back to the hotel, into the saloon, to talk to Willie. The saloon wasn't open yet, but Willie was there. He was always there. The saloon was his responsibility, and he took good care of it. He also knew that Clint and White were friends and that Clint had special privileges, so he wasn't surprised when Clint walked into the closed saloon.

" 'Morning, Clint."

"Hello, Willie."

"Something I can do for you this morning?" Willie asked. He'd been sweeping the floor, and he leaned on the broom now.

"I'm looking for McGregor."

"He's in and out," the big man said. Clint was about six-one, but he had to look up to catch Willie's eyes.

"I need him today."

Willie shrugged and said, "I'll see what I can do, Clint."

"I'll be in the hotel for the next two hours."

Willie grinned then and said, "All right."

Clint gave the big man a little salute and left, going in through the dining room. He ran into Leona, almost knocking her off her feet. Luckily her hands were empty. He reached out and grabbed her around the waist to keep her from falling.

"Whew," she said, "thanks. I saw my life flash in front of my eyes."

He held her that way, looking into her eyes, and got the same feeling he'd gotten the day before, when Linda Wentworth had been in his room with him.

He let her go.

"Are you all right?"

"I'm fine," she said, smoothing herself out, running a hand over her hair. "You weren't in for breakfast today."

"I'm here now," he said. "How about some flapjacks?"

She smiled and said, "Coming up. I'll have coffee for you in a minute."

Clint nodded and walked to his table. Some man, he thought, letting a little lady throw you.

She brought him his coffee, and over it he thought about what Wentworth had said, about the shooting being unrelated to the job. It was a distinct possibility, but that would have factored in coincidence, and Clint had factored coincidence out of his life a long time ago.

He was halfway through an impressive stack of flapjacks when Terence White came walking into the dining room. There weren't many people around at that time—breakfast was an *early* meal at the Silver Spur—and he heard the exchange between Leona and White.

"Mr. White," she said, "two mornings in a row. To what do we owe this pleasure?"

"I'm evaluating the staff," he said, and then added quickly, "just kidding, Leona."

"What can I get you?"

"I'll just have some of Clint's coffee," White said, pointing to Clint's table.

"I'll bring you a cup and a fresh pot."

"Thank you."

White walked across the room and sat next to Clint, on his left.

"Jackpot," he said.

"What?"

"Your hawk-faced killer."

"You've got something already?"

"Yep. He's a Cherokee half-breed called—get this—Lazarus."

"Lazarus was raised from the dead," Clint said.

"Well, this Lazarus puts people in their graves, and he's good."

"He missed."

"If he missed," White said, "he must have meant to—either that or you're a lot faster than I've seen . . . of late."

Leona came over and left the cup and a fresh pot of coffee, taking the old pot with her. White poured himself a cup.

"Do you know who hired him?" Clint asked.

"No, all I know is that he hit town about two weeks ago."

"Then he wasn't brought in for me," Clint said thoughtfully.

"It doesn't look that way."

Clint stopped chewing to consider, slashing at the air with his fork.

"That would explain why he'd take a job on me that wasn't a kill," Clint said. "He's already got a kill job, and he was just moonlighting."

"But for who?"

"That's what I've got to find out."

"Haven't been any big killings in the papers the past two weeks," White said. "Maybe he hasn't pulled that one off yet."

"I'd like to find out what he's here for, too."

"Getting civic-minded all of a sudden?"

Clint pointed with his fork. "If he's here to kill somebody big, and I stop him, there could be money in it."

"So much for civic-minded," Terence White said, and drank his coffee.

SEVENTEEN

"Where does he think you are?" Linda Wentworth asked.

"Running his errands," Bob Stock replied.

She turned over and ran her hand over his hairless chest, slipped one leg over him. They were at a hotel in a less than affluent part of town, where nobody would ever expect to see either one of them.

"What if he goes home and doesn't find you there?" he asked, reaching for one of her breasts.

"I'll tell him I was shopping," she said, reaching for and finding his erection and closing her hand over it. "He knows I always go shopping."

"Yeah," Stock said, pulling her on top of him, "but for what?"

Linda made a little growling noise and kissed him, thrusting her tongue into his mouth. He put one hand on each of her hips, raised her up, and brought her down, entering her cleanly and effortlessly. . . .

"Clint was at the office?" she asked later.

"This morning."

"What did he want?"

"I don't know. I was outside and they were inside."

"You didn't listen at the door?"

He frowned at her.

"I don't listen at doors, Linda."

"You'll bed the boss's wife, but you won't listen at doors?"

"Would you love me more if I did?"

"No, darling," she said, sliding her legs off the bed and standing up, "of course not."

He stared at the smooth line of her back, the firm roundness of her bare buttocks, and thought about how lucky he was. From the first moment he met her he had wanted to bed her, and when he finally got the chance he couldn't believe his luck. They'd been meeting like this for several months now.

She moved over to a straight-backed chair that was set in front of a mirror and starting fixing her face and her hair.

"Are you leaving?"

"I have to, darling," she said. "If I'm going to tell him I was shopping, I have to shop."

"We could stay a while—"

"He'll be expecting you back," she said.

"I know."

She lifted her arms and in the mirror he could see her small, firm breasts rise.

"Jesus," he said, "you're beautiful."

"Thank you, darling. Now hurry and get dressed."

"All right," he said, slipping out of bed.

They kissed before leaving the hotel room separately, first him and then her. After he was gone she wondered how much longer she could keep this up without seeing some results. She'd made an art form out of manipulating men like Bob Stock. At one time she'd worked her magic on older men, like her husband, but of late she had turned her attention to younger ones, like Stock. Old or young, though, they were easily controlled by a woman of her experience and skills.

She'd been cultivating Stock because he was closer to her husband's business than she was. He'd be able to tell her things she wouldn't otherwise know.

She was still rifling through other people's belongings.

Some things never changed—but she was trying.

She waited fifteen minutes, then left the hotel, checking her watch.

She was going to be late for her next meeting.

EIGHTEEN

After Terence White left, Clint stayed in the dining room and nursed another pot of coffee. Pretty soon he was the only one left in the room. The lunchtime crowd wouldn't start piling in for an hour, yet.

Leona came over and asked, "Anything else I can get you?"

"I'll just finish this pot of coffee, Lee."

"Waiting for someone?" she asked, cleaning the rest of the table.

"Yes."

She looked at him, caught his eye, and said hesitantly, "A woman?"

He looked at her for a few seconds and then said, "No, not a woman. I'm waiting for a man who may or may not show up."

"Oh."

"Sit down, Lee."

"Oh, I can't—"

"Sure you can," he said. "I'm the only customer, and you've got to keep me happy. Besides," he added, trying a real smile, "I know the owner."

She sat down.

"How old are you?" he asked.

She looked at him, surprised, and said, "Twenty-five."

"Have you lived in San Francisco all your life?"

"No. I was born back East. I worked my way West, starting from when I was sixteen, usually working tables—which is why I do it so well."

He believed her. Some girls who worked as saloon girls or whores to get across the country often claimed to have worked as waitresses, but he saw no hint of either saloon girl or whore in this lady.

"Are you happy here?"

"Very," she said. "I never got paid so much for waiting tables, and I've made a few friends. Do you know, I got a raise after being here only a week or two?"

He knew.

"That Terry," he said, "he really knows talent."

She frowned slightly and said, "Why are you asking me all this?"

"Just making conversation."

"Well," she said, "am I allowed to play, too?"

"Sure."

"You're not so scary, you know."

He stared at her and said, "Where did that come from?"

"All the others who work here, they think you're scary— even Highbinder, and I know he likes you."

"Who thinks I'm scary?"

"The other girls, the desk clerks," she said. She leaned closer to him and he could smell her hair, her perfume, and the perspiration under her arms. It was all very pleasant. . . .

"Did you know," she said in a conspiratorial whisper, "that you're the reason there's been such a turnover in desk clerks these past few weeks?"

"No."

"It's true," she said. "I guess you scare them the most."

"I guess I do."

"You don't try to be scary, do you?"

"No," he said. "I guess it just comes naturally."

"Well, I just want you to know, *I* don't think you're so scary."

"I must be doing something wrong, then."

"No," she said very seriously, "you're doing something right."

He was about to say something else to her when he saw McGregor. He entered from the hotel lobby. Leona saw Clint looking past her and turned her head.

"Is that the man you're waiting for?" she asked.

"That's him."

She looked at McGregor for a few moments, then turned to Clint and said, "Now, *he's* scary!"

NINETEEN

McGregor came over to the table, and Leona excused herself. He sat in the chair she'd vacated.

Clint studied McGregor for a moment. He'd never thought of the man as particularly scary-looking, but he guessed that to other people it might be true.

McGregor could have been a fighter, but he never had been. He was a big man, particularly through the shoulders and chest. He had gray hair, even though he was only in his late thirties, and a nose that looked as if it belonged on somebody else's face. He was not a handsome man and had, in fact, been described as ugly, but he never seemed to have any trouble with women. They liked him, and he liked them. Maybe that said it all.

McGregor was a handyman. When Clint needed somebody for a job in San Francisco, any kind of job, he used McGregor. The man was usually able to deliver, no matter what the request was—and he didn't come cheap.

"I hear you're looking for me," McGregor said.

Clint had never heard anyone call him anything but McGregor. Even though he knew the man's first name was Angus, he never used it.

"I need a tail."

In spite of the fact that McGregor was big and ugly, he was uncannily able to follow people without them knowing he was there.

"On who?"

Leona picked that moment to bring over an empty cup and a fresh pot of coffee.

"Thank you, lass," McGregor said.

"Sure," she said with a smile. Clint had a feeling that she didn't think McGregor was so scary anymore. It didn't usually take much longer than that for women to change their minds about him.

"Lee," Clint asked, "can you get me a piece of paper and a pencil?"

"Sure thing," she said, and produced them right there and then.

"Thanks."

Clint wrote down the name "Robert Stock" and the address of Wentworth's business on Market Street.

"This man," he said, handing the paper to McGregor. The big Scot had the coffee cup in his right hand and took the paper with his left.

"What's he done?"

"I don't know," Clint said.

"What do you want to know?"

"Who he sees."

"Anybody in particular in mind?"

"Dark man with a hawk nose."

McGregor looked at Clint and said, "Lazarus?"

"You know him?"

"I know *of* him. Is he in town?"

Clint nodded.

"Took a couple of shots at me yesterday."

"And missed?" McGregor asked in surprise.

"I think he was supposed to."

"I'd say so. If he *wasn't* supposed to, you'd be dead for sure—at least, judging from what I hear."

Something occurred to Clint then.

"How well do you know his story?"

"Just his rep."

"Does he work alone?"

"Usually. Did you see him?"

"No, somebody else described him to me."

McGregor put Stock's name and address in his shirt pocket and poured another cup of coffee.

"How close do you want me to get to this fella?" McGregor asked.

"How close can you get?"

McGregor shrugged.

"Maybe close enough to hear."

"If you can do it, do it," Clint said, "but don't get spotted."

"Usual pay?" McGregor asked.

"More," Clint said. He slid a couple of hundred across the table as a down payment.

McGregor's bushy eyebrows went up.

"You doing that well in the game?"

It didn't surprise Clint that McGregor knew about the poker game.

"No," Clint said, "I'm working for a rich gentleman."

"Not this guy," McGregor said, patting the piece of paper in his pocket.

"No, the man he works for."

"Does he know you're tailing this guy?"

"No."

McGregor nodded.

"Anything else I need to know?"

"Yes," Clint said. "If Stock meets with Lazarus, just let me know. Don't move on him. Understand?"

"Sure," McGregor said, setting the cup down empty. "That'd cost you extra, anyway."

"I know," Clint said.

"How often you want to hear from me?"

"Just when you have something to tell me."

"All right, then," McGregor said, "time to go to work. Thanks for the coffee."

Clint waved the man's thanks off and watched him walk across the room. He got to the doorway just as a man and woman did, and they both drew back from him, giving him plenty of room.

Yeah, Clint thought, I guess he is kind of scary.

Comes natural to some of us.

TWENTY

"Where have you been?" Angela Hong demanded of her brother.

"Around," Jimmy Hong said. He hadn't come home that night because he'd found a white woman who had never been to bed with a Chinese "boy" and was willing to pay for the pleasure. He had given her her money's worth, and had passed her name to a few of his friends now that she'd had a taste of yellow.

"Did you hear what happened yesterday?" she asked.

"No."

"Somebody was here, looking for one of us, I guess——"

"Who was here?" he asked sharply.

"A man, I don't know who. Anyway, somebody started shooting at him."

"Kill him?"

"He would have, but I heard somebody helped him."

"Who?"

"Jenny?"

He made a face.

"Miss Too-Good-for-Her-Own-People?" he said.

"Jenny is not like that, Jimmy."

"She is to me."

"What does that tell you?" Angela asked.

"Angela—are you still seeing that rich man's son?"

"Jack? Yes. Why?"

"Maybe his father had something to do with what happened yesterday," Jimmy said. "Maybe you shouldn't see him anymore."

"Don't be silly—"

"Angela—" he said, grabbing her shoulders.

"Let go!" she said, pulling away, rubbing her arms where he'd grabbed her. "You've changed your mind awful fast," she said. "I thought you wanted me to get as much out of him as I could."

"I changed my mind," he said. "You're my sister, and I don't want to see you get hurt."

She stared at him.

"What's wrong?"

"What do you mean, 'What's wrong'?" he asked.

"When you start playing the devoted brother, something is wrong."

"Did it ever occur to you that I just might *be* a devoted brother?"

She shook her head and said, "Never." She moved toward the door and said, "I have to go out."

"Angela—"

"I don't want to talk about Jack, Jimmy," she said to him. "Not with you."

He watched her go out.

If she wouldn't talk to *him* about Jack, she was going to end up talking to Toy Lee about him.

Or worse.

Wang.

TWENTY-ONE

"Things have changed," his client said.

"Like what?" Lazarus asked.

"I've got another killing for you."

"That's more money," the man with a hawk face said.

Lazarus was tall and painfully thin, so thin it made his nose look that much bigger. Beneath his nose his mouth was a cruel slash, thin lips almost bloodless.

"Who?"

"Clint Adams."

"The man I shot at yesterday?"

"Yes."

"I thought you wanted him warned off."

"Well, now I want him dead."

Lazarus stared at his client: well dressed, a superior look. He loved working for people like that, taking their money to do their dirty work. They thought they were better, and yet they needed someone like him.

"That's going to cost extra," he said.

"I know."

"A lot extra," he said. "There's no two-for-one discount in my business."

"I realize that."

"I'll need a down payment on this one, too."

"What about the money I paid you already?"

"That was to scare him off," Lazarus said. "I looked into this man. I could have told you he wouldn't scare."

"Well," the client said, "now he'll just have to die, won't he?"

An envelope appeared and was pushed across the table to him. There was no one else in the run-down café that Lazarus had adopted, and he took the envelope, opened it, and riffled through the contents.

"All right?" the client asked.

"For now," Lazarus said, leaving the envelope on the table. "What about the other one, the first one? When do you want that done?"

"I'll let you know."

"Waiting time costs extra, you know."

"I know."

The client stood up and walked out. Lazarus picked up the envelope again and touched the money inside.

San Francisco was turning out to be very profitable, indeed.

Lazarus had heard of Clint Adams and had asked around about him. He found that the man wouldn't be an easy target—especially after yesterday. Adams had moved pretty fast yesterday, but Lazarus was fairly sure he would have had him if he really wanted him. Now Adams was forewarned, making the job that much tougher.

Lazarus would keep that in mind when he set his final price.

TWENTY-TWO

Jimmy Hong went to see some of his friends.

They called themselves the White Powder Gang. They weren't a real tong, of course, just a gang of young men who wished they *were* a real tong. Jimmy had belonged to the gang once and still kept in contact with them.

He met with them now.

"There's a man named Clint Adams," he said. "Anybody know him?"

"I've heard of him," Danny Wing said. "He's a bad one. Supposed to be a real bad man with a gun."

"Too bad for White Powder?" Jimmy asked.

"No one is too bad for White Powder," Harry Chin said. Harry was the leader of the White Powder Gang.

The other half-dozen gang members present all nodded their heads in agreement.

"This man is after my sister."

"He want to make little yellow babies?" Jackie Chong said, laughing.

Jimmy took two steps and backhanded Chong across the face.

Chong stood up quickly, but Harry Chin said, "Stop! You deserved that. You dishonored his sister."

"*He* dishonors his own sister!" Chong said. "He talks about her all the—"

"She is *his* sister," Harry Chin said. Grudgingly, Jackie Chong sat down. Harry Chin looked at Jimmy and said, "Go on."

"He's looking for my sister," Jimmy said. "I don't want him to find her."

"How bad?" Harry Chin asked.

Jimmy looked at Chin and said, "Toy Lee doesn't want her to talk to him."

"Ah," Harry Chin said, and the others all nodded. They knew that if Toy Lee was involved, then they were to use any methods they could to keep Clint Adams away from Angela Hong.

"We get paid for this?" asked Jackie Chong.

"Didn't you hear him?" Harry Chin said. "Toy Lee does not want Clint Adams to talk to Angela. That is all we need to know."

Harry Chin looked at Jimmy Hong and said, "Tell Toy Lee he has nothing to fear."

"I will tell him," Jimmy said. "He will be very pleased."

He bowed to Harry Chin, who bowed back, and then Jimmy left the gang's headquarters, a dirty basement on Dupont Street.

Jimmy hoped that it would not get back to Toy Lee that he had invoked his name.

Maybe he shouldn't have done it, but it was too late now.

It was also too late to play the protective brother.

Maybe that's why he was doing it.

Jenny Soo felt a responsibility to the man named Clint Adams. After all, she had saved his life. It had now come to her attention that the White Powder Gang had "orders" to make sure that Clint Adams never got to speak to Angela Hong.

Her responsibility manifested itself in two ways. One, she felt she had to warn Clint Adams about White Powder; two, she felt she had to help him get to Angela Hong.

Maybe that was just because she didn't like Jimmy Hong.

She knew what was happening because one of the White Powder Gang—a young man named Jackie Chong—often came to the laundry where she worked and bragged about how important the White Powder members were.

"This time," he told her, "we've been asked by Toy Lee himself to take care of this *lo fan* who is trying to find Angela Hong."

His point was that Toy Lee thought so much of the White Powder boys that he had gone to them with this important mission.

Of course, Jenny Soo had no use for any of the White Powder Gang—especially Jackie Chong, whom she found to be simply abhorrent.

"Uncle," Jenny said after Jackie Hong left, "I have to go out."

"You go out when there is work to be done?" her uncle asked.

"I will return as soon as possible, Uncle," she said, removing her white apron, "I promise."

Her uncle, sixtyish, frail, and gray, smiled and said, "You go to see boyfriend?"

"How many times do I have to tell you, Uncle," she said to the old man with affection, "I don't have a boyfriend."

Her uncle smiled even wider and said, "You go to find a boyfriend?"

She smiled at her late mother's brother, whom she loved dearly, and said, "Yes, Uncle, I am going to find a boyfriend."

"You take time," he said, waving her away. "You take all time you need."

Toy Lee looked up from his desk as Wang entered the office. The big man had knocked so quietly that Toy Lee might have thought it was someone else, except for the fact that Wang was the only one who was *allowed* to knock on his door.

"Yes, Wang? Why are you not on the door?"

"Ki is watching the door, master," Wang said. "I have heard something I thought you should be aware of."

"And what is that?" Toy Lee said, lighting up one of his beloved American cigars.

"The word has circulated on the street that you have sent the White Powder Gang after Clint."

Toy Lee stopped rotating his cigar over the flame of his match, and the end of the cigar flamed up. He waved the match out in annoyance and dropped it in the ashtray.

"What?"

"I said the word has—"

"I heard you, Wang," Toy Lee said. "I would never use those White Powder pups to take out my garbage!"

"I know that, master," Wang said.

"This is not good, Wang," Toy Lee said, his anger growing. "I cannot have people thinking that I use . . . those children . . . and *morons* . . . to conduct my business!"

"Yes, master," Wang said. "How could such a rumor begin?"

Toy Lee frowned, taking a moment to consider, then looked at Wang and said, "Bring me Jimmy Hong."

TWENTY-THREE

That afternoon Clint went back to Chinatown to look for Angela Hong.

Walking through the streets and alleys of Chinatown, he thought that perhaps he was drawing more curious looks than usual today, but he ignored them. If these people had a problem with him being there, that was too bad. That was something they were going to have to deal with.

He went to Angela Hong's residence on Dupont Street and knocked on the door. As had happened before, there was no answer, but he didn't accept that now. He found an alley alongside the building and went to the back. There he found a window he could force, and gained entry to the building.

He found that the inside of the building had at some time been gutted and cribs had been built, single-room residences made of flimsy pinewood. Many of the doors had no locks, and most of the "rooms" were empty, the occupants probably out working for whatever meager living they could earn. The rooms that were inhabited had to be the ones that were closed and secured somehow from the inside, maybe by a piece of

wood or some piece of furniture pushed up against the entrance
by the occupants.

There were four floors made up of these rooms, and the
owner of the building was probably earning a fortune from
rents. There was just no way Clint could possibly tell which
room belonged to Angela Hong.

He retraced his steps to the back of the building and went
out through the same window by which he had entered.

As he turned away from the window he found himself facing
three young men, all Chinese and all grinning.

"You like to break into other people's homes, *lo fan*?" one
of them asked.

Just what he needed, he thought, a Chinatown citizens' com-
mittee. He kept his hand away from his gun, because he didn't
want to prompt them into any kind of action. Clint was by no
means a fast gun, and if they all made a move against him
there was no way he'd be able to take out all three of them.

"I made a wrong turn," he said, watching the three of
them. They didn't look at all like concerned citizens. They
looked like Chinatown hoods, probably members of some
gang.

"Hey, the *lo fan* is funny," the spokesman said. "We are
supposed to laugh," he told his companions, but then he looked
at Clint and said, "but we are not laughing."

The spokesman said something to one of the men and he
suddenly took his hand from behind his back. He was holding
a small gun, and pointed it at Clint. It looked like a Derringer
he might have stolen from some woman's purse, but it was
just as deadly at this range as Clint's Colt.

"What do we do now?" Clint asked. "You fellas want my
money?"

"No," the spokesman said, "no money, *lo fan*. We want you
to stop looking for Angela Hong."

"Angela Hong," Clint said. "Are you her brother?"

The spokesman started laughing.

"I wish I was her brother. Then I'd be able to peek at her
when she was getting dressed."

The other two laughed, but the gun one of them was holding never wavered. Clint continued to keep all of them in view, even though he felt no one would move until the spokesman—the leader—did.

"Then what's your relationship to her?" Clint asked.

"She's Chinese," the spokesman said, "and we're Chinese, and you, my friend, are *lo fan*. That's the only relationship we need to have."

"What do you want from me?"

"I told you," the man said, "we want you to forget about seeing Angela Hong."

"And if I don't agree?"

"You won't walk out of this alley," the spokesman said. "As a matter of fact, even if you *do* agree, you aren't going to walk out of this alley."

"Then why should I agree?"

"Not only will you agree," the spokesman said, "but you will crawl and say anything else we want you to say by the time we're through with you."

Clint laughed at them, and the leader frowned as the laughter grew louder.

"If you think I'm afraid of three yellow punks, one with a pop gun and one with a big mouth—and I don't know what this other fella has behind *his* back—you're entirely wrong. You fellas want to tangle with me, you come on ahead, because I've got other things to do and other people to see."

They were set up in a semicircle around him, no more than two giant steps of Clint's long legs away from him. Clint started to laugh again, and when the other two men looked to the leader for guidance, Clint took those two giant steps and slapped the little gun out of the gunman's hand. He swept his arm outward, toward the mouth of the alley, so the gun would arc away from the three of them.

He found out then that the three of them were pretty fast in their own right. As he pulled his gun, the leader suddenly kicked out, catching him on the wrist. His hand went numb as the gun spun through the air away from all of them.

Now he found out what the third man had behind his back as he brought a long knife into view. It had a smooth and slender blade, and Clint could see that it was razor-sharp.

The three of them closed on him, and Clint knew he wasn't going to come out of this without some damage—if he came out of it at all.

TWENTY-FOUR

The only place that Jenny Soo knew she could look for Clint was in front of Angela Hong's building on Dupont Street, because she had no idea where Clint lived or where his office was, if he even had one. Thanks to Jackie Chong she knew that the big *lo fan* was looking for Angela, whom Jenny knew well, so she went to Dupont Street, ready to settle down in front of the door and wait.

As she approached the building she passed the alley next to it and became aware of some activity inside. She entered the alley and saw Clint backed against a wall, facing three of the White Powder Gang. In that moment she realized that Jackie Chong was not with them.

Suddenly they leapt at him and she saw the flash of a knife. She heard the sound of fists and feet landing, and then she saw a flash of red as the knife did its work.

She kicked something and looked down. It was a gun, a big Colt, probably Clint Adams's. She knew that if she didn't do something they were going to kill Clint, so she picked up the gun. She'd never held one before, but the principle wasn't hard to figure out. She pointed it, holding it in both hands, closed her eyes, and pulled the trigger. The recoil jolted her wrists and pushed her a couple of steps back. She didn't know if she had hit anything, but she closed her eyes, steeled herself, and fired again.

Only then did it occur to her that she might accidentally hit Clint Adams.

TWENTY-FIVE

At the sound of the shot, Clint immediately allowed his knees to buckle, and he went to the ground. He knew he had sustained some injuries—and hoped that he had dished out some in the exchange—and that he might sustain more putting himself down on the ground like that, but *somebody* was firing a gun, and the ground was the safest place to be when that was happening.

A second shot must have found its mark, because he heard someone grunt. A voice said something in Chinese, and they each took a kick at him—two of them finding their mark—before the three men took off down the alley. He watched from the ground as they ran into the girl who was standing there, possibly not realizing that she had been the one firing at them. The girl was spun around and dumped unceremoniously on her butt.

Clint pushed himself to a seated position and proceeded to take stock of his condition. His left sleeve was soaked with blood from a neat slice in his forearm. Something was in his eye, blocking his vision, so he assumed that his head was bleeding from some kind of injury, possibly a kick.

"Are you all right?"

He looked up and saw the girl.

"You're making a habit of saving my life," he said.

He started to get up and she caught him under the arm to try to help him, but he was too heavy and had to do it himself. On his feet he leaned back against the wall and felt his ribs. They were sore, but he didn't think any of them were broken.

"How did you know where to find me?" he asked. He took the gun from her and holstered it.

"I didn't," she said. "That's why I came here."

"Run that by me again?"

"I had something to tell you, and I didn't know where to find you, so I thought I'd come here and wait for you," she explained.

"You knew I'd come here?"

"You would if you were looking for Angela Hong."

"And how did you know that?"

She looked at his arm and the blood dripping from it to form a puddle on the ground and said, "Can we go someplace where I can bandage that?"

"You got a place?"

"My uncle's laundry."

"Lead the way," he said. "Your credit is perfect with me so far."

TWENTY-SIX

It was not a long walk to the laundry owned and operated by Jenny's uncle. Along the way Clint managed to find out that Jenny's last name was Soo and that she worked for her uncle.

"Do you live with him, too?" he asked.

"I have my own room above the laundry," she said.

The difference between that and living with him seemed to escape him, but he did not comment on it.

When they reached the laundry, Clint saw that it was a small place with no sign saying what kind of establishment it was, but he could smell the steam even on the street.

Inside, an old Chinaman with a lined face and watery eyes looked up at them from behind the counter, and he smiled, revealing yellowed teeth—what there was of them.

"Ah, you find boyfriend?" he said.

"He's not my boyfriend, Uncle," Jenny said patiently.

"Not boyfriend?" the old man asked.

"No," Jenny said.

The old man looked at Clint's bloody sleeve and said, "He say no and you cut him?"

"I'll be in the back, Uncle, bandaging his wound. If anyone asks, we are not here."

"Fine, fine," the old man said, bobbing his head, "you no here."

"Come on," Jenny said, and led Clint behind the counter into a back room.

"Sit," she said, and he sat in a flimsy wooden chair.

She rummaged around for bandages, left the room for a moment, and when she returned it was with a basin of water. She placed it on a table next to him and said, "Give me your arm."

She tore the sleeve away, revealing the clean slice. The blood didn't seem to bother her as she cleaned it, and then she began to wrap a bandage around it.

"You might have to go to a doctor to get it closed properly," she said, "but this should keep you from losing too much blood until you do."

After she had securely bound it she took the basin away, disappeared, and returned without it.

"Can we talk now?" he asked.

"We could have talked while I bandaged you."

"I didn't want to break your concentration."

She pulled over another chair and said, "Let's talk."

"You don't mind if I reload while we do," he said, taking out his gun.

"Not if it won't ruin your concentration."

He ejected the empties and inserted fresh cartridges as he said, "What was it you wanted to tell me?"

She grinned ironically and said, "I wanted to warn you that you might run into some trouble with the White Powder Gang."

"The White Powder Gang? What is that, a tong?"

"They'd like to be," she said, "but right now they're just a group of young men who think they're tough and that they'll run Chinatown someday."

"How did you know they were after me?"

"One of them is after *me*," she said, "and he was in here bragging."

"Well," he said, "at least he's got good taste. I appreciate the warning, but can you tell me *why* they're after me?"

"To keep you from finding Angela Hong."

"I know that," he said. "But why?"

"The boy I spoke to—his name is Jackie Chong, by the way, and he wasn't one of the three you were fighting with—told me that Toy Lee had asked them to help him keep you away from her."

"Not likely."

"Why not?"

"Toy Lee wouldn't use a bunch of amateurs to do his dirty work."

"You know Toy Lee?"

"Very well," Clint said. "We have a healthy respect for each other."

"Then if he didn't send them after you, who did?" she asked.

"That's what I'd like to find out," he said. "You wouldn't know where to find this Jackie Chong, would you?"

"I know the White Powders have a . . . headquarters in a basement on Dupont Street, but I don't know exactly where it is," she said. "Sorry."

"Don't be," he said. "You've already done more for me than I have any right to ask."

"You didn't ask," she said, "so my help is still available."

"Why?"

"Why what?"

"Why risk yourself helping me?"

"Well, the first time I did it because you were in trouble, and I couldn't see just leaving you there. The second time I did it because—well, I like Angela Hong, and I dislike the White Powder boys. Can you accept all of that?"

"Sure," he said. "They're as good reasons as any I've ever heard."

"Can you tell me something?"

"What?"

"Why are you looking for Angela Hong?"

"Just to talk to her."

"About what?"

He frowned, then decided that she had earned the right to know. He told her about Samuel Wentworth and his concern that Angela might be after his money.

"That's nonsense," Jenny said.

"Why?"

"Something like that would never occur to Angela. She's just not the type."

"I see."

"Now, her brother's another story."

"Jimmy Hong?"

She nodded.

"He's got that kind of devious mind, but Angela doesn't listen to Jimmy so much anymore."

"Why not?"

"When they were younger and their parents died, Jimmy accepted the responsibility of taking care of Angela, keeping them both alive. When she got older, she discovered that she didn't like the things Jimmy was doing to keep them surviving."

"Things like what?"

"Oh, running with the White Powder Gang, sleeping with white women who had never had a Chinese boy and were willing to pay."

"Like a whore?" Clint said. "A *male* whore?"

"Exactly like that."

"So if Jimmy wanted her to milk Jack Wentworth for money, she wouldn't do it?"

"No."

"Do they live together, still?"

"Yes, but Angela wants to get away from him."

To Clint that had a connotation different from the one Jenny meant it to have.

"I know what you're thinking now," Jenny said.

"Do you?"

"Yes, that Angela sees Jack as a way to get away from Jimmy."

"And she wouldn't see it that way?"

Jenny thought a moment.

"No, to be honest, Angela is smart enough to figure that out, but knowing her I would say she really loves Jack Wentworth."

"You say you know her."

"Very well."

"Has she ever talked to you about Jack?"

"No. We know each other—and like each other, almost like a younger and older sister—but we don't see each other that often anymore. We're both . . . trying to survive in our own way."

"Does she work?"

"Yes. There's a place in Chinatown where girls and women sew for cheap pay. Naturally, it is owned and operated by a *lo fan*. She works there."

"A white man owns a business in Chinatown?"

She smiled.

"Although he doesn't pay much, he pays, so he is left alone to run his business. Without him girls like Angela might end up . . . elsewhere."

Clint knew that she meant working the streets as a whore, or one of the whorehouses.

"Would you be able to take me there?"

"Sure," she said, "as long as you promise me that you mean Angela no harm. You're not going to try to threaten her, are you?"

"That's not what I was hired to do," he said.

"What exactly were you hired to do?"

"To find out if she really is after the Wentworth money."

"And how do you intend to do that?"

"I intend to ask her."

"And you'll believe what she says?"

"I'll believe what her eyes and face tell me," he said. "I tend to know when people are lying to me."

"That must be a wonderful talent to have."

"Not always," he said. "Can we go now?"

"Don't you want to see a doctor?"

He held up his arm and flexed his fingers. The arm hurt, but he said, "I'm fine. I'd like to get this job over with."

"What about the White Powder Gang?"

"I have a feeling that a certain old Chinese gentleman—and I use the term loosely—will be taking care of them," Clint said, "as soon as he gets the word."

TWENTY-SEVEN

Jimmy Hong knew he was in trouble.

The first time Wang had come for him he had simply said that Toy Lee wanted to see him. This time Wang took him by the neck and marched him forcefully over to Toy Lee's office.

Jimmy knew he was in trouble, and he thought he knew why. One of those White Powder fools had opened his mouth trying to impress some China doll.

On the way to Toy Lee's he tried to come up with a reasonable explanation for what he had done.

Now, standing in front of the old man, he wasn't quite confident in the story he'd come up with.

Toy Lee waited patiently for Wang to bring Jimmy Hong to him. Not only was he embarrassed to have his name connected with the White Powder Gang, but also if the gang succeeded in harming Clint Adams or worse, killing him, Toy Lee would never be able to regain the respect he would lose. Most of the people Toy Lee did business with knew of his uneasy truce with Clint Adams. If they thought that the truce had been broken by Toy Lee, they would cease doing business with him because they would then deem him untrustworthy.

Toy Lee had to do something that would wipe this embarrassment from his name without question.

In the past such decisions had been easy. The body of a man who had embarrassed him would be found hanging from a streetlamp in Chinatown, and his head would be found hanging from a lamp on the Barbary Coast.

That was an old-time method, however. These were more modern times and called for more modern methods despite how attractive the older method sounded to him at the moment.

Jimmy waited for Toy Lee to dismiss Wang, and when he didn't he knew he was in *serious* trouble.

"You have embarrassed me," Toy Lee said simply.

"Toy Lee, please—"

"You have been a constant source of disappointment to me, Hong Soo, ever since the unfortunate death of your beloved parents," Toy Lee said, using Jimmy Hong's Chinese name.

"You mean ever since they were murdered."

Toy Lee closed his eyes and waved the distinction away gently. He knew how bitter Jimmy was against the *lo fan* for what had happened to his parents, but that was not at issue here.

"Do not attempt to change the subject," Toy Lee said.

"I can explain—"

"When I have outlined the form of embarrassment," Toy Lee said, "you can explain. You have apparently allied yourself with those fools who call themselves the White Powder Gang." Toy Lee said the name with contempt. "Fools, morons, amateurs! Further, you have circulated word that I have asked for their help, through you."

"I can explain—"

Jimmy saw Toy Lee nod slightly, and then a sledgehammer—or something like it—struck him on the back of the neck. He staggered forward and fell to all fours. Shaking his head, he started to get up.

"Stay there!" Toy Lee commanded, and Wang's foot came down on his back, not a blow, just to keep him where he was until Toy Lee was finished.

"When you left those White Powder fools I thought you had become smart, but you have not. By connecting my name with theirs you have caused me embarrassment that is immeasurable—and may be irreversible. Now," Toy Lee said, waving so that Wang's foot was removed from Jimmy Hong's back, "what have you to say for yourself?"

Jimmy Hong struggled to his feet and stared at Toy Lee. His story went through his mind, and even to him it seemed lame, foolish. Aware of Wang behind him and knowing that the big man could have killed him with a harder blow to the neck—or in a dozen different ways—he said the only thing he could think of at the moment.

"Don't kill me."

TWENTY-EIGHT

Clint followed Jenny Soo to the place she'd been talking about—the sewing shop, or whatever it was called. The door was open, and he followed her inside.

The heat inside was oppressive, like walking into an invisible wall. Immediately he felt the perspiration form on his forehead.

"Jesus," he said, "how can they stand it?"

"They can't," Jenny said. "Some days some of them are carried out. They have water thrown on them to revive them, and then they are brought back in."

Clint looked around and saw no windows. In fact, there *had* been windows at one time, but they had all been boarded up.

"Why doesn't he open up the windows again?" he asked.

Jenny laughed.

"*He* boarded them up in the first place."

Clint used his right sleeve to wipe the sweat from his brow, but he could feel it forming in the small of his back, too.

"Do you see Angela?"

"No, but something's wrong."

"What?"

"I don't know, but the women look frightened about something."

Clint looked at the women sitting at their posts. Some of them had sewing machines, but most of them seemed to be working by hand. They were all looking at him and Jenny, trying to do so without *seeming* to do so.

"Talk to them, Jenny."

"Yes."

Jenny approached some of the women and spoke with them, then returned to Clint looking worried.

"Well?"

"Angela was here, but shortly after she arrived three men broke in and took her away."

"Three men? What men?"

Jenny stiffened her jaw and said, "White Powder."

"What the hell did they take her for?" he wondered aloud.

"Because you want her."

That made sense to Clint. They hadn't been able to finish him, so they had come here and taken Angela so he wouldn't be able to find her.

"This is crazy," he said. "All I want to do is talk to the girl, and now her life might be in jeopardy."

"What can we do?"

He looked at her and said, "You can go back to your uncle's laundry."

"And you?"

"I'm going to go and see Toy Lee," Clint said. "Maybe he can go about getting her released without anyone getting killed."

"Do you think they'd kill her?" she asked, looking alarmed.

"I don't know," he said, "but I know that if I have to go after them, *I'm* going to end up killing some of *them.*"

TWENTY-NINE

Clint went directly to Toy Lee's establishment in Ross Alley. When the little slide in the door opened it was not Wang's eyes he was looking at.

"I want to see Toy Lee."

"Who you?" a voice asked.

"Clint Adams."

He could see that the name meant something to the owner of the eyes.

"You wait."

The slide closed and Clint had to wait longer than he had ever waited for Wang. Eventually the eyes reappeared and the man said, "You come."

The door opened and he found himself looking at a smaller version of Wang. This man was not as big, but he was impressive just the same. Clint followed him down the familiar route to Toy Lee's office. The gambling room was just starting to fill up, with people and with smoke.

The man knocked on Toy Lee's door and then admitted him.

"What happened to Wang?" Clint couldn't resist asking. "He get fired?"

"He is on an errand," Toy Lee said. "Ki is his brother."

"That doesn't surprise me."

"I believe I know why you are here."

"Oh, yeah? Why?"

"White Powder."

"Yes."

"You are here because of the . . . word on the street?"

"I know better than to believe that you'd use rank amateurs like that, Toy Lee. You have more respect for yourself than that, and I have more respect for you than to believe it."

Toy Lee bowed his head in thanks and said, "How can I help you?"

"About White Powder," Clint said. "they've taken Angela Hong."

Clint was surprised by the old man's reaction. The veins and tendons of his scrawny neck stood out and for a moment Clint thought the man was going to scream, but when his voice finally came it was low and calm—with an underlying tension.

"What?"

"They went to the place where she works and took her out."

"Why?"

"They must have figured I'd find my way there. I only want to talk to the girl, Toy Lee, you know that. I mean her no harm."

"I know."

"I don't know if *they* mean her any harm."

"I will take care of it," Toy Lee said.

"Will you see to it that I get to speak to her?"

Toy Lee hesitated and for a moment Clint felt that, even though Toy Lee had not solicited the services of the White Powder Gang, he might *not* have wanted Clint to speak to her for some reason.

"We will speak of that when I have secured her freedom."

"Who started all of this anyway, Toy?"

"An unfortunate soul," Toy Lee said, "who took much upon himself and paid for it."

"Is that the errand Wang is on?" Clint asked. "Making sure that he pays?"

"No," Toy Lee said—almost sadly, Clint thought. "I have taken care of the matter myself."

"You? How?"

"An old custom, borrowed from our Japanese brothers," Toy Lee said.

He touched a linen cloth on his desk and pushed it across to Clint's side of the desk. Carefully Clint unfolded it, then drew his hands back when he saw what had been folded up in it.

Somebody had recently lost a little finger.

THIRTY

Clint returned to the Silver Spur after leaving Toy Lee. He was going to skip the poker game tonight, even though he knew that someone would be taking his seat and he might not get it back for days—if ever. He just didn't think he would be able to concentrate on the cards.

Before leaving Toy Lee's he had broached one more subject.

"Someone tried to kill me in Chinatown, Toy," he'd said.

"White Powder?" Toy Lee asked.

"They tried today," Clint said, showing Toy Lee his tightly bandaged wrist, "but that's not the attempt I'm speaking of."

Quickly he told Toy Lee about his first meeting with Jenny Soo—not mentioning her by name, though—and how she helped him get away from his assailants.

"I have since discovered that the man's name is Lazarus."

"A hired killer?"

"Yes, but brought here to San Francisco for someone else, not me. I think he was sent after me as an afterthought."

"Why do you tell me this?"

"I'd like to find out who Lazarus is here to kill," Clint said. "I'd also like to find out who was with him when he shot at me."

"And you think I know these things?"

"I think you know people," Clint said, "who might know these things."

Toy Lee thought a moment and then said, "We will speak of this another time as well."

Clint accepted that and left.

When he entered the lobby of the hotel he saw Jenny Soo sitting there. Her shoulders were hunched, her hands were between her knees, and her head was down as she stared at the floor. Clint knew why. No one there would have made her feel welcome.

He walked over to her and said, "Jenny."

She looked up at him with great relief and said, "Clint!"

"What are you doing here?"

She stood up and said, "I was worried about Angela. What happened?"

"I spoke to Toy Lee and he'll see that she's released."

She closed her eyes and said, "Good." She looked at his sleeve and said, "Haven't you seen a doctor yet?"

"No," he said, lifting it and looking at it. Blood had started to seep through the bandage.

"You should see one," she said, "or you will have a nasty scar."

"It won't be my first," he said.

"What else did Toy Lee say?"

"He seemed quite upset. Listen, are you hungry?"

She smiled and said, "I am always hungry. Why?"

"Come on, I'll buy you dinner."

He grabbed her hand and started to lead her to the dining room, but she held back.

She lowered her voice and said, "Here?"

He released her hand and turned to face her.

"Sure. Why not here?"

He looked around and saw that several people were standing in the lobby, staring at them. He caught the clerk staring, gave him a scary look, and the man quickly looked away.

"Come on, Jenny. . . ." he said.

"They do not like me being here," she said, shaking her head and looking at the other people.

"Who?"

"Anyone."

"So?" he said. He leaned over and said in a low voice, "They're a bunch of snobs. Let's rub their faces in it. What do you say?"

She looked at him doubtfully, and then slowly the dubious look on her face was replaced by another. She looked like a little girl who had agreed to do something mischievous.

"All right," she said, taking a deep breath, "let's eat."

Clint had to give Leona credit. When she came over to take their orders she never flinched once when she saw Jenny.

Clint ordered steaks for both of them, and Leona smiled at them and went to fill the order.

"Is she your woman?" Jenny asked.

Clint looked at her.

"Now, what would make you ask a question like that?"

"The look in her eyes," Jenny said, "the way she looks at you. You have not noticed?"

"No," Clint said.

"Perhaps it takes another woman to notice. You like her, don't you?"

"I don't—well, sure, she works here, she waits on me every day—"

"You like her as a person."

"Well . . . sure. Listen, Jenny—"

"This kind of talk makes you uncomfortable?"

"Not uncomfortable," he said, "just—"

"You are a man who is not used to letting his emotions show. You wish to present a . . . a hard surface, that you are a cold man."

"Jenny—"

"I know differently."

"Jenny, I thought you wanted to hear what else Toy Lee had to say."

She stared at him a few moments, and then with an amused half smile on her face said, "Very well. We will talk about Toy Lee."

After dinner he walked her to the front door and said, "Will you be able to get back all right?"

"Yes, I am used to traveling on my own."

"What about your uncle?" he said. "Won't he be worried about you?"

She laughed.

"What's funny?"

"When I left he said, 'You go to see boyfriend?' "

"What did you tell him?"

Shyly she said, "I did not have the heart to tell him no. Do you mind?"

"No," he said, "I don't mind."

There was an awkward moment between them and then she touched his left arm and said, "See a doctor in the morning."

"I will," he said. "I promise."

"If you need my help you know where I am."

"The first life-threatening situation I encounter," he said, "I'll come running."

"Thank you for dinner."

"You're welcome."

Finally, having run out of things to say, she stepped out onto the boardwalk and started walking away. He watched her until the darkness had swallowed her up, and then went back inside.

When he turned to go upstairs he caught Leona watching him from the entrance to the dining room. Having been caught, she did not duck out of sight quickly, but simply nodded to him and went back inside.

He went upstairs, wondering why women confused the hell out of him when he could see everything else so clearly.

•   •   •

He was getting ready to turn in when there was a knock at the door. He decided not to try to guess who it was and just opened the door.

"Hello," Jenny said.

"Forget something?" he asked.

"May I come in?"

"Sure."

She moved past him and he closed the door and turned to face her.

"How did you get past the lobby?"

"The man at the desk saw me with you earlier. I told him you were expecting me."

"I see."

"Were you?"

He frowned at her and said, "No," and then realized what she was getting at.

"Then maybe I should leave," she said, starting past him.

"Jenny—" he said, taking hold of her arm.

"If you don't want me to stay," she said, "maybe I am just making a fool of myself. Maybe you . . . don't like Chinese girls."

"It's not that."

"Then what?" she asked. "The girl in the dining room?"

He hesitated a moment and then said, "No, there's nothing between her and me."

"Maybe I should be more forward, then," Jenny said, turning to face him. "With your luck you might be dead soon."

"That's a cheerful thought."

"If that happened I would never see you again," she said. "I would not like that." She put her arms around his neck—he had to bend to help her—and said, "I would not like that at all."

THIRTY-ONE

Clint cupped her buttocks in his hand and lifted the naked Chinese girl, holding her tightly to him. Her breasts were crushed against his chest, and her flesh was very hot. Her mouth was eager on his neck and face, and then starving as it covered *his* mouth.

He turned and walked to the bed with her and lowered both of them as gently as he could, without breaking the kiss.

When he moved his mouth down over her neck to her breasts she moaned and arched her back. He nibbled at her nipples, and them moved lower still, using his tongue, his lips, and his teeth. When he entered her with his tongue, she gasped and lifted her buttocks off the bed, her belly trembling. He slid his hands beneath her, cupping her surprisingly plump buttocks again, and held her there while he worked on her with his mouth. She was not as light as she had seemed dressed. Her breasts *and* buttocks were pleasant surprises, full and firm for a girl so small. He had always heard that Chinese girls were not well endowed, but Jenny Soo was not of that mold.

He continued to minister to her with his mouth until she could no longer take it. When she began to drum on his

back with her heels he lowered her to the bed, raised himself over her, and entered her, swiftly, almost brutally. She
was very wet and slick, and he slid in easily. She raked his
back with her nails, and bit him on the shoulder to keep from
screaming. . . .

Across the street from the Silver Spur, in a darkened doorway, the man who called himself Lazarus had watched as Clint
turned and went back inside. It never occurred to him to follow
the Chinese gal and do her any harm. He wasn't getting paid
for her.

He'd managed to find out that Clint was playing in a big
poker game being held in a private room in one of the fancy
Portsmouth Square hotels. He decided that he would wait until
Clint left to go and play his game.

He'd never get there.

Angus McGregor watched the lighted window of Robert
Stock's room. He'd been standing across the street for a few
hours, ever since he'd followed Stock home from dinner. The
man had dined alone, and had returned home alone without
making any other stops.

The man lead a boring life from what McGregor could see,
but tomorrow was another day.

He left his doorway and started home himself.

Robert Stock was thinking about Linda Wentworth. He was
thinking about the feel of her skin, the taste of her mouth—
her very talented mouth which almost drove him crazy when
it touched him . . . there!

Embarrassed, he looked down at the bulge in his pajama
pants. The erection had come unbidden, and there was nothing
he could do about it. Sometimes, when he thought of her at
work, he swelled and was then embarrassed to get up from
his desk.

He knew that Linda had a problem and that she was probably waiting for him to ask if he could help her. He *would*

have, gladly, but he was afraid he knew what her problem was.

Robert Stock didn't know if he was ready to commit murder—not even for Linda Wentworth.

But—oh, God!—he didn't want to lose her.

Linda Wentworth sat on her bed, her hands folded in her lap. She was waiting for her husband to come to bed. No, actually, she was *dreading* the moment when he would come to bed. Although Samuel Wentworth had kept himself in good shape for a man his age, she still disliked the feel of his rough, wrinkled body on hers. She much preferred the feel of a young man's body—a young man like *Jack* Wentworth.

She knew that Jack felt the sexual tension between them, just as she did. If only she could get his mind off that damned Chinese girl.

If she could only get rid of that girl!

Jack Wentworth stared out the window of his room, which was in his father's house. It was time, he thought, to find a place of his own, so he could take Angela out of Chinatown.

He was worried. She had not met him that night like she was supposed to. He knew that there could be any number of reasons why she had not shown up, but he was worried anyway, thinking the worst.

Chinatown was such a filthy hellhole. What if something had happened to her? She was always telling him that Chinatown was her home, that nothing could happen to her there.

He wished he could believe her.

Samuel Wentworth wondered for the thousandth—maybe the millionth—time whether he had done the right thing in hiring Clint. Perhaps, when the man had told him how he'd been shot at, he should have told Clint to forget the whole thing—but he couldn't. If there was a chance that the shooting was connected with the job Clint was doing for him, did that mean that Jack was in danger, too?

Oh, how he wished he could just go up to his bedroom and enjoy the feel of his young wife. He knew he'd been neglecting her lately, but she was so understanding. She knew he was under a lot of pressure.

She was the only bright spot in his life right now.

Angela Hong was confused.

She was alone on a dark Chinatown street, still trying to get her bearings. Only minutes earlier she had been a prisoner of the White Powder Gang, her brother's own gang. They had never told her what they wanted of her, and now they had simply released her.

She had to find Jimmy to see if he knew what was going on.

Jimmy Hong's hand hurt where the bottom of his missing finger had been.

He couldn't believe that he had accepted the knife Wang had handed him and had willingly—no, *eagerly*—cut off his own finger and offered it to Toy Lee. He couldn't believe that Toy Lee had made him do that!

But he was grateful to be alive and given a second chance. Toy Lee could just as easily have had Wang cut his throat with the same knife. He'd been given a second chance and intended to make the most of it.

This time he would make no mistakes.

Toy Lee sat behind his desk, the burning cigar forgotten in his hand. He knew that Clint Adams would be coming back the next day for some answers and he knew that the man would not leave without answers.

He had to decide what to tell him, because the truth was out of the question, and he had a feeling that Clint Adams knew the truth when he heard it.

Toy Lee, though, had grown up lying, and after so very many years of doing it, he was quite good at it.

In fact, he was *excellent* at it.

• • •

Jenny Soo sat up in bed and stared down at Clint Adams, studying him as he slept.

She envied that *lo fan* waitress in the hotel dining room for being able to see Clint every day, *wait* on him every day.

So many times she had tried to talk Angela Hong out of her . . . her *involvement* with the *lo fan* Jack. She had told Angela many times that she was only looking for trouble getting involved with a white man.

Now, suddenly, she understood.

THIRTY-TWO

Lazarus was upset with himself.

It had never occurred to him that Clint Adams might *not* go to the poker game tonight, even when he saw the Chinese girl leave and then return.

That was foolish. He had wasted a lot of time waiting out here, and now it was late, after 1:00 A.M.

Lazarus stepped out of the doorway and wondered how surprised Clint Adams would be if Lazarus showed up in his room. Everything Lazarus had heard about Adams told him that the man was dangerous.

It would have been a challenge to try to get into his room and then wake him up by cutting his throat. It took a man a few minutes to die from a slit throat. He would have had time to look into Clint Adams's dying eyes and said, "Your throat's just been cut."

A challenge, all right—a foolish one.

There was too much money to be made here to mess it up by fooling around with a dangerous man.

Tomorrow, when Clint Adams was out in the open, he'd finish him.

Right now he wanted to get back to his own hotel room on the Barbary Coast. He had one of those Barbary Coast sluts waiting there for him, the kind who would do anything—*anything*—for money.

They would have a lot in common.

Clint woke and saw Jenny's dark outline seated next to him in bed.

"What are you doing?" he asked.

"Watching you."

"In the dark?"

"My eyes are used to it," she said. "I can see you."

Slowly his own eyes got used to the dark and he could make out the features of her lovely face. He rolled over and put his hand on her hip. The skin was smooth and warm, as it had been when he'd run his mouth over it hours before.

"What's wrong?" he asked.

She shrugged and said, "Maybe I just want to talk."

"So talk," he said, stroking her hip. "I'm a good listener."

So she started to speak, telling him how she had come to this country with relatives after both of her parents had died in China. Her father had died first, of pneumonia, and her mother months later. Jenny believed that she had died of a broken heart.

She was an only child, and her aunt and uncle had taken her with them when they left China with their own child and came to the United States.

"The golden mountain," she said, shaking her head. "That's what everyone used to call this country. We heard stories about people getting rich here, taking gold right up out of the ground."

"It's true," Clint said, "but it's not that easy."

"That's what we found out when we got here," she said. "My aunt and uncle worked hard, and my cousin and I both worked when we got old enough. She was a year older than I was."

"Where are they now?"

"My aunt was killed. Like many Chinese women she had to go to work in a whorehouse, and one night a man beat her to death."

"And your cousin?"

"She ran away," Jenny said. "She just . . . ran away one day, ten years ago."

"And it's been your uncle and you ever since?"

"Yes," she said. "We both worked hard and saved money, and eventually my uncle opened his laundry. That was four years ago."

"What about you, Jenny?"

"What do you mean?"

"I mean, did you ever . . . uh, I mean . . ."

"You mean, did I ever go to work in a whorehouse? It's all right, you can ask me that. Yes, I did, but all I did was clean it," she said. "I did most of my work cleaning other people's homes."

"It's a cleaner job," he said.

"I know," she said.

"So now you work with your uncle?"

"Yes," she said, "until Mr. Right comes along."

She didn't say that as if she believed it.

"Don't you think there is a Mr. Right out there for you, Jenny?"

"With my luck," she said, "you are Mr. Right."

"Jenny—"

"And if I am correct, you don't think you are anyone's Mr. Right."

"I'm just not the type, Jenny."

"I know," she said. She slid down under the covers so she could snuggle up close against him. Her full, firm breasts pressed pleasantly against his chest, and her mouth was on his neck.

"I guess I will just settle for what I can get."

He put his arms around her and said, "That's all any of us can do."

She lifted one leg over him, then moved to straddle him. She lifted her hips, reached between them for his erection, and then lowered herself onto it slowly. She let her breath out slowly as he filled her, and then she braced her hands on his chest as she rode him wetly.

Clint closed his eyes and ran his hands over her as she moved on top of him. Her tempo increased and continued to increase until she was coming down hard on him, gasping and crying out as he pierced her deeply, and then she almost screamed when he exploded inside of her. . . .

THIRTY-THREE

Clint was stiff the next morning.

He groaned as he got out of bed and studied himself in the mirror. He had bruises all around his ribs on both sides. He had a cut on his scalpline that was hard to see, since it had scabbed over. The real problem was his wrist, though. It was swollen and stiff, and the blood had soaked through the makeshift bandage he had put on it before going to bed. Jenny had left his room an hour before, and it was a wonder he'd been able to perform the way he had with her. Then again, she had spent most of her time on top, riding him, being careful not to hurt him, and the sex had certainly taken his mind off his other aches.

Now that everything hurt, though, he wondered if his damned wrist was broken.

His first stop would be to see Doc Boyer.

"What did you do to yourself this time?" Dr. Carl Boyer asked him.

"I didn't do anything to myself," Clint said. "I got it done to me."

"Where?"

"Chinatown?"

Boyer looked at Clint as he probed his wrist.

"Don't you ever learn?"

"I'm working on something, Doc."

"Chinatown is a bad enough place to go when you're playing," Boyer said. "I'm going to have to sew this thing up, but you should have come to see me right away. You're going to have a nice scar. Not a bad one, because the knife was apparently sharp."

Clint sat patiently while the doctor gathered up the tools he needed, and then watched as the man sewed him up.

"I don't have too many patients who actually watch me do this," the doctor commented.

"It's my arm," Clint said. "I want to make sure you do it right."

"Hmm."

"Is it broken?"

"No," Boyer said, "just badly bruised and abused—abused, like the rest of your body. You've got more scars than any man I've ever seen."

"I lead an interesting life."

"Yeah, well, I don't have time to hear about it."

"That's good," Clint said, "because I don't have time to tell it."

"Good."

There was silence between the two men who *could* have become friends if either of them had time to try it, and then the doctor asked, "How are you doing in the big poker game?"

"I lost my seat last night."

"Small wonder."

"How did you know about the game?"

Boyer looked at Clint and said, "A lot of people know about the game, Clint."

"Where did *you* hear about it?"

"From one of my patients."

Clint frowned. If so many people knew about the game, what was to stop Lazarus from trying for him when he was going to or coming from the game?

Had the man been waiting for him the night before, unaware that he was not going to the game.

He hoped he had.

He hoped Lazarus had waited into the wee hours of the morning for him to come out of the hotel.

"There," Boyer said. "Take it easy on that wrist for a while. You're right-handed, aren't you?"

"Yes."

"Then you're lucky it was your left arm that got cut."

"Luck had nothing to do with it, Doc," Clint said, rolling his sleeve down.

"You mean—yes, I believe you do mean it," Boyer said. "I'd hate to find myself in a situation where I'd have to think as quickly as you obviously do, Clint. I'd end up dead."

"Maybe you underestimate yourself," Clint said, standing up. "Everyone has an instinct for survival that takes over in a bad situation."

"Reach up over your head," the doctor said, and proceeded to check Clint's ribs. "They don't seem to be cracked. You can close your shirt. I suppose you're right about the instinct for survival in us all, but I hope never to have to find out for myself how good mine is."

"I'd put my money on you," Clint said.

"I appreciate that, Clint."

In Clint's book, any man who could sew another man up, or dig a bullet out, or take a baby from its mother without killing either, would have an excellent instinct for survival— for others as well as for himself.

Clint paid the doctor and thanked him for his care.

"I've already seen you twice too many times this week, Clint," Boyer said. "Do me a favor: Make sure the third time is in a saloon somewhere, over a drink."

"I'll work on that, Doc," Clint said. "I'll work on that."

After leaving the doctor's office he went to the Silver Spur dining room for a cup of coffee. Curiously, he wasn't hungry this morning. Another man might have felt faint, or ill, after having been sewn up, but Clint had simply lost his appetite.

"Breakfast?" Leona asked, coming up to the table.

"Not today, Lee," Clint said. "Just coffee."

She frowned and asked, "Are you all right?"

"Yes. Why?"

"You look pale."

"I'm fine."

"How's your wrist?"

He looked at his wrist and then back at her.

"I noticed it last night, when you were here with that—with your friend."

"It's fine," he said. "Doc Boyer just sewed it up."

"Ah," she said, as if that explained everything. "I'll be right back with the coffee."

"Thanks."

As Clint waited for the coffee he mapped out his day. First he was going to have to talk to Toy Lee, to find out if Angela Hong had been released by the White Powder Gang. If she had, he was going to have to see if the old Chinaman was prepared to let him speak to her.

If he wasn't, it would raise some very interesting questions.

Clint wanted to talk to Angela Hong, and if she was the kind of girl Jenny Soo said she was, then he'd just report back to Samuel Wentworth that she wasn't after his money. After that, Wentworth could just worry about his son marrying a Chinese girl. That would certainly damage his standing in San Francisco society, and that wouldn't break Clint's heart. As far as he was concerned, those high society types could use some lumps; maybe that would bring them back down to earth some.

Once the job was out of the way he would be able to concentrate all his efforts on finding the hired killer known as Lazarus.

That was something else he had to ask Toy Lee: whether the old Chinaman had gotten a line on Lazarus. Clint had to repay

Lazarus for supplying Clint with one of the few moments of real panic in his life, those moments that he was without his eyesight.

That was an overdue debt Clint Adams *had* to repay before he'd be able to put those terrifying moments behind him for good.

THIRTY-FOUR

When Lazarus woke he found the slut lying on him. The night before, he'd been excited by her big, floppy breasts and heavy thighs and avid mouth. This morning he was disgusted by her weight on him. He heaved her up and pushed her so she fell off the bed.

"Hey—" she shouted, hitting the wooden floor.

"Get dressed and get out!" he said.

She sat up, peering at him through bleary eyes. They had shared a bottle of whiskey, which probably explained why he didn't remember her being so homely.

"Don't you want a little waker-upper?" she asked.

"I want you to get your floppy tits and fat ass out of my room."

"Well, that ain't no way to talk—" she started to say, but he slapped her across the face, leaving the imprint of his fingers there. The blow made her bite her cheek, and she shouted and spat blood.

"Jesus Christ, you cut me!" she said.

"If you don't get out of here I'm gonna cut your floppy tits right off."

"My man will—"

"If I see your pimp I'll stuff your tits into his mouth and then cut his throat."

Lazarus reached under his pillow and brought out a knife. It had a thick, flat blade that was razor-sharp on one side and serrated on the other.

"Now, move!" he said with a growl, showing her the knife.

"Jesus," she said, standing up and dressing quickly, "you're crazy. You know that?"

Dressed she stood up straight, wiped the blood from her lips with the back of her hand, and demanded righteously, "What about my money?"

"It's on the dresser, bitch," he said. "Take it and get out."

She walked over to the dresser, took the money off, counted it, considered complaining about the amount, and then decided that she was lucky to be getting away from this crazy man with her tits still attached.

She left in a hurry.

Lazarus leaned over and spat on the floor, then swung his feet to the hardwood floor and scratched his crotch. He stood and dressed quickly without washing, strapped on his gun, and left the hotel.

He wanted to get to the Silver Spur nice and early. There was no sense letting Clint go on wondering when it was going to come.

THIRTY-FIVE

Toy Lee called Wang in early that morning and gave him his instructions.

"And take Ki with you," he added as Wang was leaving.

"Yes, master."

Toy Lee had confidence that both Wang and Ki would be back before Clint arrived.

Jimmy Hong found the White Powder Gang in their basement. They were about to greet him when they saw the gun in his hand.

"Hey, are you crazy?" Harry Chin asked.

"Which of you talked?" he asked.

"What?" Chin asked.

"One of you bragged to someone that you were all working for Toy Lee," Jimmy Hong said. He brought his bandaged left hand out from behind his back and showed it to him. "I had to give Toy Lee one of my fingers to appease him."

Jackie Chong stared at Jimmy Hong in awe and said, "You gave him one of your fingers?"

"Cut it right off and gave it to him," Jimmy Hong said. He was aware that some of them were looking at him with renewed respect. It was a respect he had not received since his days as leader of the gang.

"Now I want to know who bragged," Jimmy Hong said.

"Why?" Chin asked. "What does it matter? It's done, isn't it?"

"No," Jimmy Hong said, "it's not done."

"What do you want, Jimmy?" Harry Chin asked as the others watched their present leader face their former leader.

"I want to know who the braggart is."

"Why? You gonna kill him?" Harry Chin asked. "You were White Powder once, Jimmy. You know we don't kill each other—ever!"

"I don't want to kill him."

"Then what?"

Jimmy studied all of their faces. If he was any judge, the braggart was either Jackie Chong or Danny Wing. Not Harry Chin—never Harry Chin.

Chong and Wing were sitting together, so he looked right at them as he said, "He owes me a finger."

Jackie Chong's eyes almost rolled up inside his head.

It took some time for Harry Chin to convince Jimmy Hong *not* to take a finger from Jackie Chong.

Finally, Jimmy Hong put his gun away and said, "I don't want to take it, I want him to give it to me."

Danny Wing laughed, a high-pitched sound.

"Not much chance of that," Harry Chin said.

"Then until he does, he is dead to me," Jimmy Hong said.

"That is up to you, Jimmy."

Jimmy Hong looked at them all one more time and then said, "You no longer have any obligation to me. I will take care of my sister without you."

"That is up to you, too," Harry Chin said.

Jimmy Hong nodded and then left, washing his hands now and forever of the White Powder Gang.

After Jimmy left, Danny Wing said aloud, "I wonder what he's gonna do when he finds out we took his sister yesterday."

"Nothing," Harry Chin said. "We let her go, didn't we?"

"Only after we got the word that Toy Lee was angry," Ricky Hom said.

"Well, we didn't hurt her, did we?" one of the others, Tommy Sing, said.

"No, we didn't," Harry Chin replied "We have nothing to fear from anyone for taking her. We were just trying to help."

Jackie Chong laughed and said, "I was just trying to get my hands on little Angela Hong."

Harry Chin was about to say something when they all heard a door slam.

"Jimmy!" Harry Chin called. "Is that you? You coming back to apologize?"

There was no answer.

They heard somebody walking, and all the members of the White Powder Gang stood up.

"Who is it?" Harry Chin demanded.

No answer.

They all waited while the footsteps got closer, and then two massive forms came into view.

"Jesus," Jackie Hong said. "It's Wang . . ."

They all knew what that meant.

"Wait—" Harry Chin shouted in horror, but his words were cut short by a knife that flew through the air and pierced his throat.

"God, no—" Jackie Chong cried out. He turned to run, but a knife buried itself to the hilt in his back.

Two of the others—Danny Wing and Ricky Hom, who had been in the alley with Harry Chin when they had attacked Clint—clawed for the guns in their belts, but they were too slow.

They were all too damned slow.

When Wang and Ki left the basement of the building on Dupont Street—each carrying a sack—there was no more White Powder Gang.

THIRTY-SIX

By the time Wang and Ki had returned, Toy Lee had decided to use something he rarely used when dealing with the *lo fan*. He decided actually to try the truth.

The eyes looking out at him were very definitely Wang's.

"Toy Lee is expecting me."

Wang continued to stare at him for a few long moments. Then the slide closed and the bolt on the door was thrown.

"Come," Wang said.

When Clint entered Toy Lee's office, Wang closed the door, leaving the two men alone.

Toy Lee looked up from behind his desk.

"We are adversaries, you and I," Toy Lee said.

Clint frowned, not knowing what Toy Lee was up to with that kind of preamble.

"We have been," Clint said.

"Not friendly adversaries," Toy Lee said, "but then, we have never . . . never dealt in hate."

"I don't hate you, if that's what you mean," Clint said. "You've never given me any reason to."

"And I feel the same," the frail man said. He leaned his elbows on his desk and folded his hands. "That is why I feel I must be frank with you."

Clint moved forward and sat in the chair facing the desk.

"I'd appreciate that, Toy Lee."

Toy Lee held up one hand, showing Clint a long, bony index finger with a long nail.

"If what I say ever leaves this room," he said, wagging the finger back and forth, "everything I have just said will become null. I will have Wang kill you, tear off your head, and defecate in it."

"That's clear enough."

"Good."

Toy Lee once again folded his hands on the desk. Clint gave the old man a moment to form his thoughts.

"Angela and Jimmy Hong are my niece and nephew," Toy Lee said. "Their mother was my sister."

The first thought that came into Clint's mind was, and you took Jimmy Hong's little finger?

"Why is that such a secret?"

"It is a well-known fact that I have no family," Toy Lee said. "I have taken great pains to make sure that is a well-known fact."

"So your enemies can never strike at you through your family."

"Yes."

"But . . . as long as we're speaking frankly?"

"Go ahead."

"If Angela and Jimmy are so close to you, how could you take your nephew's finger?"

Once again Toy Lee showed Clint his own finger.

"That," he said, "was a matter of honor between two men. It had nothing to do with family. It is something I learned from a Japanese friend."

"I see."

"Angela has always been nearer to my heart," Toy Lee admitted. "That is why I have ensured that the White Powder

Gang will never bother her again."

Clint didn't bother asking what that meant. He thought he knew.

"And Jimmy?"

Toy Lee sighed.

"Jimmy has been a constant source of disappointment. Never—until recently—embarrassment."

"Why did he have the White Powder Gang grab his own sister?" Clint asked.

"He did not," Toy Lee said. "Let me explain. When you first came to see me I asked Jimmy to make sure that Angela had nothing more to do with Jack. Also, I did not want you to question her."

Clint picked it up from there.

"He went to the White Powder Gang and told them to make sure I didn't find Angela, and invoked your name."

"Correct."

"He didn't realize what lengths they'd take to ensure that."

"I'm sure he knew they might kill you," Toy Lee said, "but he had no idea they would take Angela."

"What was his connection to White Powder?"

"Up to a few years ago, he was their leader."

"And what's he done about Jack Wentworth?"

"I do not know," Toy Lee said. "I expect he has spoken to Angela without results."

"Would he kill Jack Wentworth?"

Toy Lee thought a moment.

"He might."

"You're not sure whether he could kill?"

"Under the proper circumstances," Toy Lee said sagely, "anyone could kill."

"To please you, he would?"

"Yes."

"Would he have the money to hire it done?"

"No," Toy Lee said. "You are speaking of the hired killer Lazarus?"

"Yes. Have you found out anything about him?"

"No. He seems to have gone to ground successfully."

"But you don't think Jimmy could have hired him?"

"No. If he went to White Powder to take care of you, it is fairly obvious he has nothing to do with Lazarus."

"That's true."

"I am sorry I cannot locate Lazarus for you," Toy Lee said. "I can keep trying. All I can assure you is that he is not in Chinatown."

"I appreciate your frankness, Toy Lee," Clint said, rising. "No one will ever discover through me that you have any family."

Toy Lee simply nodded his thanks.

Clint started for the door, then stopped and turned back.

"Toy Lee, why did you not want me to speak to Angela?"

"I—you have a certain reputation, Clint. I did not—I was not sure how you would handle her. Also, I did not want her to say something that might . . . give away her relationship with me."

"Toy Lee, if you assure me Angela Hong is not after the Wentworth money," Clint said, "that is what I will tell my client."

"You will no longer seek to talk to her?"

"I will take your word."

"Then I give it," Toy Lee said. "She is genuinely in love with this young *lo fan*. I do not approve, but . . ." He ended the statement with a shrug.

"Will you call Jimmy off and let her make her own decision?"

"Yes," Toy Lee replied "but only because the entire situation seems to have too many facets. By removing Jimmy, perhaps I will make it easier for you to find out who is behind Lazarus."

"I am in your debt, Toy Lee."

"Your silence pays the debt, Clint," Toy Lee said. "We are even."

Clint inclined his head in semblance of a bow and left.

THIRTY-SEVEN

When Clint returned to the Silver Spur Hotel there was a policeman waiting in the lobby. Clint was well acquainted with Inspector Alex Saxon, having gone head to head with the inspector on several occasions. Seeing the man, he was reminded of what Toy Lee had said about their being adversaries—not friendly and not unfriendly, just adversaries.

Much the same could be said of him and Alex Saxon.

Clint had stopped at Samuel Wentworth's office first, to give him the news. . . .

"How do you know she's not after my money?" Wentworth demanded.

"I have certain assurances in which I put a lot of credence."

"I want to know who—"

"Look, Mr. Wentworth, as far as I'm concerned the job you hired me to do is done, and you don't have to pay me another cent."

"Why not?" Wentworth asked, eyeing Clint shrewdly. "Have you been paid off by someone else?"

Clint moved closer to the man's desk, leaned on it, and bent so close to Wentworth that the man tried to burrow into the back of his chair.

"What?" Clint said.

"I apologize."

"If you checked me out you know that I don't take payoffs. When I get hired to do a job, I do it."

"Yes, I understand," Wentworth said, "but—"

"But nothing," Clint said, straightening up. "Face facts. Your son and the girl love each other. Try helping him instead of giving him a hard time."

Clint walked to the door and left. In the outer office he gave Robert Stock a brief glance and then left.

Across the street he saw McGregor, and crossed over to join him.

"Clint," McGregor said, nodding.

"What have you got on this fella Stock?"

"He's boring," McGregor replied, and gave Clint an idea of how the man spent his days and nights.

"That's it?"

"So far."

"You mind staying on?"

"Nope."

"I just lost my client."

McGregor shrugged.

"I'll get paid," the man said.

"Okay," Clint said. "Maybe one more day."

"Whatever."

"Thanks. I'll see you."

McGregor nodded and turned his attention back to the building across the street.

Angus McGregor had more patience than any man he knew.

Clint crossed the lobby, and Saxon, spying him, rose to meet him. Saxon was a little taller than Clint but slender, with bony shoulders and a slight stoop, so that the difference in height was hardly noticeable. He was in his early forties, with a shock of silver running through his dark hair. To Clint he looked more like a schoolteacher than a policeman.

"Clint."

"Inspector," Clint said. "You have some business with me?"

"Just some questions."

"Mind asking them over some food? Not that I'm trying to bribe you."

Saxon let a small smile loose on his mouth, then chased it.

"I'll have some coffee while you eat."

Both men went into the dining room and settled down at Clint's table. Clint gave Leona his lunch order, and she returned quickly with a pot of coffee.

"What's on your mind, Inspector?" Clint asked when both men had a cup of coffee in their hands.

"Lazarus."

"I know the name."

"Seems to me you know more than the name," Saxon said. "You've been asking around about him."

"Have I?"

"You know, I'll never understand your relationship with Toy Lee, but apparently he's been making inquiries for you," Saxon said.

"We . . . cooperate from time to time. But it's interesting that you'd know that."

"When Toy Lee starts making inquiries, I make it my business to find out why."

"All right, I'm looking for Lazarus."

"To hire him?"

"Saxon, you don't know me well, but I think you know me well enough to know that if I wanted somebody dead I'd kill him myself."

"True," Saxon conceded. "So then why are you looking for him?"

"He took some shots at me the other day."

"Where?"

"Chinatown."

"You saw him?"

Clint shook his head.

"He was identified for me."

"Reliable source?"

"Very."

"Why does he want you?"

"Why does he want anyone?"

"Who *hired* him to get you?"

Clint stared at Saxon and said, "If you find out the answer to that one I'd like to know it."

"Are you giving me everything on this?"

"Believe it or not," Clint said, "I've told you everything I know."

Saxon finished his coffee and set the empty cup down.

"All right," he said, "I'm going to believe you—for now."

"I'm touched."

Saxon stood up, started to leave, then stopped.

"Oh, Adams, what do you know about the White Powder Gang?"

"Not a lot," Clint said, deciding not to play ignorant. He doubted the policeman would believe it, anyway. "I hear they're a bunch of amateurs who'd like to be a powerful tong."

"Not anymore," Saxon said. "We just found their bodies in their basement hideout." Saxon looked hard at Clint and said, "Their *bodies*—not their heads."

Clint recalled what Toy Lee had said about making sure they never bothered Angela Hong again. Wang, he thought, and his brother, Ki.

"You wouldn't know anything about that, would you? I mean, since we're being so honest and straightforward with each other?"

"Inspector," Clint said, "I can honestly say I don't know who killed them."

And he didn't *know* for sure, he only suspected—*strongly* suspected—that Toy Lee had sicced Wang and Ki on them.

Clint watched Saxon walk out. Technically he was as honest

with the inspector about the White Powder Gang as he was about Lazarus.

He didn't *know* who had killed them and cut off their heads—he *suspected,* but he didn't know.

THIRTY-EIGHT

Clint loitered in the saloon for the next few hours, nursing a couple of beers. His next move was not crystal clear. He needed a line on Lazarus before he could do that. Either that, or . . .

Or he could question the principals in the Wentworth job to see if he couldn't shake a confession out of one of them that they had hired Lazarus.

That would mean talking to Samuel Wentworth again, then Jack Wentworth, Linda Wentworth, and Robert Stock. He took Toy Lee's word that he hadn't hired Lazarus; and that neither of the Hongs—Angela or Jimmy—had done so.

Before going to see them, he went over it in his mind to see if he could figure it out.

If Samuel Wentworth hired Lazarus, *who* did he hire him to kill? His wife? For what reasons? He certainly wouldn't hire him to kill his own son. Angela Hong? If that were the case, why hire Clint to talk to her? It didn't make sense that Wentworth would have done it.

What about Linda Wentworth? She could have hired Lazarus to kill Angela so Jack wouldn't marry her and produce a potential heir. She wouldn't want to split her pie with any-one. Or she could have hired him to have Jack killed for the same reason. Or her husband—again, for technically the same reason—money! If her husband was killed, she'd stand to inherit at least half his estate, wouldn't she? Good motive, indeed. Also, it had been Clint's experience that men did their own killing, and women got other men to do it for them—one way or another.

Now, what about Jack Wentworth? Who would he have wanted killed? His father, so he could inherit, and so the old man wouldn't interfere with his and Angela's plans? No, that didn't sit well with Clint. His father's wife, so *he* wouldn't have to share the pie? Somehow, Clint didn't think so, but he didn't know Jack, so he'd have to talk to him before he could really form an accurate opinion.

Robert Stock? He was out as far as Clint was concerned. No motive.

At that moment McGregor walked into the saloon and brought with him a motive for Robert Stock.

Clint stood across the street from the hotel where McGregor said Robert Stock and Linda Wentworth were having them-selves a "romantic tryst."

"A romantic tryst?" he had repeated. "You sound like quite a romantic yourself, McGregor."

McGregor had eyed him over his beer and said, "Don't you believe it."

Now they both waited outside the hotel. One would tail Robert Stock, the other Linda Wentworth.

"I've got Mrs. Wentworth," Clint had said.

"How did I guess?" McGregor replied.

"Linda."

"Hmm?"

A long pause and then, "If you want me to do it, I will."

"Do what, darling?"

Another long pause.

"K-kill him."

"Kill who?"

"Don't play games with me!" Stock said. He sat up in bed so abruptly that he literally shoved her head from his shoulder.

She sat up and put her hand on his shoulder.

"I'm not playing with you, Bob," she said, "truly I'm not. I only want you to know exactly what you're getting into—what *we're* getting into. Now please, darling, for me . . . say it."

He looked at her beautiful face, felt her hand on his belly as it moved even lower, the warmth of her glorious breast pressed against his arm and said, "I'll kill Samuel. I'll kill your husband for you."

She leaned over and kissed him gently as her hand closed around his penis.

"Not for me, darling," she said into his ear, "for *us*!"

Robert Stock was the first one to leave the hotel. He did not look like a man who had just slept with a beautiful woman. There was a mournful, worried look on his face.

"There's my man. See you at the hotel," McGregor said, and Clint nodded.

Clint had to wait another ten minutes for Linda Wentworth to leave. She looked beautiful, fresh from her "romantic tryst."

Sex seemed to agree with her. She was glowing. Or maybe there was another reason.

He gave her a small head start and then followed.

Lazarus watched Clint follow the woman, gave him a head start, and then followed him.

This was getting interesting, and he wanted to see where it would lead.

THIRTY-NINE

Clint was disappointed when Linda Wentworth went straight home. He was hoping that maybe she'd meet her hired killer.

Once Linda Wentworth was safely in her house, Clint decided it was time to talk to her. He gave her about fifteen minutes to get settled, then walked to the door and knocked.

It took a few moments for her to answer. Maybe she was worried it was her lover. He saw her look out the front window, moving the lace curtain aside, and then she came to the door and opened it.

"Well," she said, looking Clint up and down, "to what do I owe this pleasure?"

She had changed from the severe suit she had been wearing when she left to a simple dress that covered her from head to toe. Unbidden, the vision of her naked body sprang into his mind.

"I'd like to talk to you about something, Mrs. Wentworth."

"About the job you're doing for my husband?"

"That's finished."

"Is it?" she said. "Did you see it through to a successful conclusion?"

"As far as I'm concerned," he said. "Could we talk inside?"

"Sure," she said, smiling at him invitingly. "Why not? Come in."

He entered, waiting while she closed the door, and then she showed him into the living room.

"Coffee? Whiskey? Anything?"

"No, nothing, thank you."

"Just conversation?" she asked. Her tone said she hoped not.

"That's it," he said. "Just conversation."

She pouted.

"That's a pity."

He decided to throw her off guard right from the beginning.

"You can save the seduction routine for Robert Stock, Linda."

He had to admire her. Nothing showed on her face, and there was just he barest flicker of her eyes when he said Stock's name.

"I beg your pardon?"

"Robert Stock," he said. "Your husband's assistant? And your lover!"

She stood there with her mouth open, as if she didn't know what to say, and then finally said, "That's totally absurd!"

"Is it?" he said. "I just followed you from the hotel where you had what a friend of mine called a 'romantic tryst.'"

"A . . . friend of yours?"

"Yes," he said, "a man I had following Stock."

"Following Robert? Whatever for?"

"I wanted to see if he was meeting with a hired killer."

"I . . . don't quite understand this," she said.

"It's easy. There's a hired killer in town. I don't know exactly who he was brought in to kill, but while he was here someone sent him after me. Now I figure he's working for one of four people: your husband, your stepson, Stock . . . or you."

"Me?" she asked. "Why would I need a hired killer?"

"Maybe you want to inherit your husband's money without waiting for him to die a natural death. Or maybe—"

"Maybe you had just better leave!" she said coldly. "I wanted my h-husband k-killed—how could you suggest such a thing?"

He stared at her in awe. There were even tears in her eyes.

"You're going to tell me you love him?"

"Of course I love him," she said.

"That's why you're sleeping with his assistant?"

"I'm sleeping with Robert Stock—if it's any of your business—because my husband can no longer give me what . . . what I need. He is much older than I am. I thought we went through this in your hotel room."

They had gone through that . . . and a lot more.

"Of course," he said, "that's why you made my acquaintance at the Alhambra and slept with me."

"You approached me at the Alhambra," she said, "remember?"

"You agreed readily enough," he said, "*and* came back again."

She smiled at the memory and said, "Yes, I did come back. I only meant to talk to you that second time, but as you might recall, things got carried away."

"Yes, they did. Were you sleeping with Stock before me?"

"Yes," she said, "but if you must know, Clint, you'd be my first choice—if I were picking a permanant lover, that is."

"I'm flattered."

"Don't be," she said.

He had to hand it to her. She hadn't lost control, and she hadn't given him anything he could use.

Except maybe . . .

"How do you think your husband would feel if he found out about you and Stock? Or you and me?"

"I see," she said, her tone filled with disgust. "Now you want money to keep quiet."

"I don't want your money, Mrs. Wentworth."

"What then? Me? Again?"

She was too fast for him then. She undid her dress in record time and discarded it. Apparently Linda Wentworth felt no need for underwear when she was at home. A very progressive woman—and a beautiful one. She cupped firm breasts, flicked the dark nipples. She had a trim waist, and full hips that tapered into almost perfect thighs and slender calves.

"Have me, then," she said. "Come on, let's see what a real man you are. Take me in my own house!"

She was breathing heavily, and her nipples were distended. She really *did* want him to take her—and he couldn't deny wanting to, right at that moment.

Clint stared at her and knew that she could get a man to do anything she wanted him to—*most* men.

"I'm sorry to have disturbed you, Mrs. Wentworth," he said, and turned to leave.

"What?" she said, gaping in disbelief. "You're leaving?"

"Yes," he said, "I'm leaving."

"But . . . but even after . . ." she stammered, falling speechless.

Apparently no man had ever turned her down before—not while she was naked and willing—no, not just willing, positively eager.

"Yes," he said, "even after seeing all you have to offer. You see, Linda, I don't dally with married women. Good day."

As he went through the front door he heard a high-pitched "ooh!" of frustration, and something struck the other side of the door.

When he got outside it suddenly occurred to him why Robert Stock might have looked as mournful as he looked when he left the hotel.

He hailed a horse-drawn cab and told the driver to hurry to Samuel Wentworth's Market Street business address.

Lazarus cursed.

After Clint Adams jumped into the horse-drawn cab the killer had not been able to find one for himself.

He'd lost Adams.

He looked at the Wentworth house, shrugged, and went up the steps.

He'd just have to do Clint second.

When Clint reached Wentworth's office he saw McGregor standing across the street and hurried to join him.

"Come on," Clint said. "We got to get inside."

"Why?"

"When did Stock go in?"

"A few minutes ago."

"It took that long to get here?"

"He stopped at his rooms first."

"For what?" Clint asked. McGregor was hurrying to stay with him as they crossed the street.

"I don't know—"

"Could it have been a gun?"

"I don't—wait, he had his hand in his jacket when he came out, and seemed nervous."

"I think the lady talked her lover into killing her husband— unless we can stop him!"

The two of them hurried up the stairs to Wentworth's office. As they entered they didn't see Stock at his desk. That meant he had to be inside, with Wentworth.

At that moment they heard a shot.

FORTY

"Tell me how you figure this?" Inspector Alex Saxon said to Clint.

Clint looked down at the body on the floor. . . .

At the sound of the shot Clint had pulled his gun and hit the door with his shoulder. The door burst open and he and McGregor piled in, guns ready.

What they saw surprised them.

Wentworth was sitting behind his desk, holding a gun loosely in his hand.

Stock was on the floor, bleeding from a hole in his chest. His eyes were fluttering and, as Clint watched, the man died. Next to him was a gun he'd obviously been holding when he'd been shot.

"The stupid fool was going to kill me," Wentworth said to them.

Clint looked at Wentworth and said, "That's what I figured."

"I got him first," Wentworth said, looking at his gun. "I— I keep this in my top drawer—I knew—I mean, in case . . . I, uh, I got him first. . . ."

"I can see that," Clint had said.

• • •

Minutes later Clint looked at Saxon and said, "The wife and the assistant were having an affair. She got him to agree to kill her husband, and he came over here to do just that, only the husband got him first."

"And how'd he do that?"

"According to what Wentworth told me, Stock was too nervous to do it right away. He kept talking, apologizing. Wentworth asked if he could have a cigar, when Stock said yes, he opened his top drawer—"

"—and produced a gun instead of a cigar," Saxon said. "That's the same statement we been getting out of him."

"What about the wife?" Clint asked.

"We've got nothing to tie her to this," Saxon said, "but I've sent a man to her house to get her."

Clint chewed his lip.

"I guess this means that Lazarus being in town has nothing to do with this family, or the job you were doing, huh?"

"I'm not so sure," Clint said.

"What? Come on, Clint. The wife got the lover to do it. She didn't hire Lazarus."

"Maybe somebody else did?"

"Who? The lover? Why would he come here to do it himself? You thinking about the son?"

"No," Clint said.

"But that only leaves . . ." Saxon said, frowning. He looked into the outer office, where one of his colleagues was talking to Wentworth for the fifth time. "You think he hired Lazarus? What for?"

"When we came in he said he kept the gun in his top drawer, and then he started to say 'I knew—' and stopped short."

"What was he going to say?"

"Maybe that he knew about the affair?"

"If he knew, you figure he hired Lazarus to kill the lover? That would have been ironic, if the lover had gotten him first."

"Maybe he hired Lazarus to kill the wife first," Clint said.

"Bring a hired killer in from out of town to kill his wife? There's plenty of guys right here in San Francisco who would have done the job a lot cheaper."

"He's a wealthy man," Clint said. "Wealthy men only hire the best."

"Like he hired you?"

Clint just stared at Saxon.

"And speaking of that, if he hired Lazarus, then he sent him after you. Why'd he do that?"

"I don't know," Clint said, "but that's something I'd like to find out."

"Well, he's not going to tell you," Saxon said. "If you're right and he's behind Lazarus, then he's not going to say so. He's been giving us the same story verbatim for the past twenty minutes."

"Like he rehearsed it?"

"Just like he rehearsed it."

"Saxon," Clint said, "let's take him to his house."

"What for?"

"To check on his wife. Maybe if we put them face to face, something will happen. Especially after she finds out her lover's dead."

Saxon thought a moment, then said, "That could be interesting. Let's do it."

When they arrived at the Wentworth house—Clint, McGregor, Saxon, Wentworth, and two other police officers—the man Saxon had sent ahead was waiting out front.

"Inspector, am I glad you're here," the man said.

"What's the matter, Davis? Can't get in?"

"No, sir," the young officer said nervously, "I got in, all right."

"And the lady was there?"

"She was there, all right," he said, "in her bedroom. Uh, Inspector—"

"Come on, boy, spit it out! She kick you out of her bedroom?"

"She couldn't very well do that, sir."

"And why not, Davis?"

"Uh, because she's, uh, she's dead . . . sir!"

FORTY-ONE

Linda Wentworth had been violently raped and then stabbed—or the other way around. There was really no way to tell for sure.

Samuel Wentworth either broke down at the sight of his wife's body sprawled on their bed, or gave a pretty good performance of a grieving husband.

Saxon had one of the officers take the sobbing Wentworth downstairs while he, Clint, and McGregor remained in the bedroom. The other officers were out in front of the house, keeping anyone from entering.

"Well?" Saxon said, looking at Clint. "Now what?"

"We've got to figure Lazarus did this."

"Sure, but how do we prove it? And how do we find out who he's working for?"

"He's working for the husband," Clint said. "I'm sure of that now."

"How can you be sure?"

"I can feel it."

"Well, that's fine, but I can't arrest a man on the basis of what you feel."

155

"I feel it, too," McGregor said.

"Great," Saxon said. "I can't do anything with your feelings, either."

McGregor shrugged and said, "I just thought I'd throw them in."

"Thanks."

"Lazarus is still going to come after me, though," Clint said.

"What?" Saxon said, turning from McGregor to Clint. "Why?"

"The wife is dead and the lover is dead, but he still has to come for me."

"If he's smart he'll get out of San Francisco before I get my hands on him," Saxon said. "Anyone who would cut up a beautiful woman—"

"He'll come for me," Clint said. "He will. A man like him, he *has* to."

"So we put a couple of men on you—" Saxon started to say.

"No," Clint said, "no police. You'll just scare him off."

"You want to take him on alone?" Saxon said.

"Do you know another way?"

"Well," Saxon said, "if worse comes to worst, I can always arrest him for killing you."

"He won't," McGregor said.

"And you won't," Clint said.

"You hang yourself out there with a target on your back," Saxon said, "and I will. Bet on it."

Clint poked Saxon with his index finger and said, "You've got a bet."

FORTY-TWO

Clint returned to the Silver Spur Hotel with McGregor, warning Saxon to stay away and to keep his men away.

"I don't want you hedging your bet," Clint said.

"Clint," Saxon said, "this is probably the only bet I ever made that I hope to lose."

"Saxon," Clint said, "I almost take that as a compliment."

When Clint and McGregor were in the dining room with a pot of coffee in front of them McGregor said, "What do you plan to do?"

"Wait," Clint said, "just wait."

The waitress, a woman named Edwina, came over and asked if she could bring them anything else.

"No, nothing, thanks," Clint said. Leona had the night off, which was just as well. He didn't need the extra added distraction.

"You're just going to sit and wait for Lazarus to come for you?"

"What else can I do?" Clint asked. "It's useless to go out and look for him. He's killed Linda Wentworth now, he knows the police will be looking for him."

"Then he should leave town."

"He should," Clint said, "but he won't."

"Why not?"

"Would you?"

McGregor thought it over a moment, then said, "I think I would."

"That makes you smarter than he is," Clint said, "or me, because I wouldn't."

"I'm just not as prideful as the two of you, I guess."

"No," Clint said, standing up, "you're smarter."

"Where are you going?"

"To my room."

"To sit and wait."

Clint nodded.

"Where do you want me?"

Clint shrugged.

"Go to the desk and tell them I said to give you a room."

"And then what?"

Clint grinned at him and said, "And then get some sleep. Your part is finished."

Clint was sitting in his chair. If he had to wait for someone to come to try to kill him, he might as well wait in comfort.

When the knock came at the door, he stood up. Maybe Lazarus was going to be polite about it.

"Excuse me, I hate to disturb you, but I'm here to kill you."

Clint palmed his gun and went to the door.

"Who is it?"

"Leona."

"Wha—"

He pulled the door open and yanked her into the room, closing and locking the door behind her.

"What the hell are you doing here?" he demanded.

She pulled her arm from his grasp and said, "I thought we should talk."

"About what?"

"About you being such a tough, confident man when it comes to everything but women. Or is it just me?"

"Leona—"

"Maybe there's something about me you don't—"

"Lee!"

"What?"

"I don't have time for this right now."

"I see," she said, looking around the room. "You're doing something very important? Reading, perhaps?"

He made a futile hand gesture with his gun hand and she saw the weapon.

"Is . . . something wrong?" she asked, suddenly realizing that he had answered the door armed.

"Yes," Clint said, "any minute I'm expecting a man to come here and try to kill me."

"What?" she said. "What are you—"

At that point there was another knock at the door. He held his left index finger to his lips and motioned for her to get behind the bed. She hurried over and crouched down behind it, peeking over it.

"Who is it?" Clint asked, pressing his back to the wall next to the door.

"Jimmy Hong."

"What?" Clint said aloud.

"Jimmy Hong!" Jimmy said louder.

"Jesus!" Clint said. He unlocked the door, yanked it open, pulled the man in, then closed and locked the door. "Now, what are you doing here? I thought Toy Lee told you—"

"He's got my sister, Adams."

"Who's got her?"

"Lazarus."

Clint studied Jimmy Hong for a hint of deception.

"When?"

"He took her tonight. He said you're to come, alone, to get her."

"Where?"

"The basement where the White Powder Gang had their meetings."

Clint rubbed his jaw. Leona stood up, studying both men with a puzzled look on her face.

"Why would he grab her?" Clint asked himself.

"Because," Jimmy Hong said, "she was with Jenny Soo . . . and he grabbed her!"

Jimmy Hong insisted on coming along.

"If I show up with you," Clint said, strapping on his gun, "he'll kill both of them."

"He won't see me," Jimmy Hong said.

"Look, Jimmy, this is the wrong time to play the dutiful brother."

"You're wrong, Adams," Jimmy Hong said. "This is the right time."

"I can't take you—"

"There's a secret passage in that basement," Jimmy said. "With the whole White Powder Gang gone, I'm the only one who knows about it."

Clint again studied Jimmy Hong's face.

"If you're lying to me—"

"I'm not."

"All right," Clint said, "wait for me outside."

Jimmy Hong nodded and went out into the hall.

Clint turned to Leona and said, "Lee—"

"Forget it, Clint," she said. "Go and do what you have to do. But remember, we have unfinished business."

He smiled at her—a real smile—and then went out into the hall.

"All right, Jimmy," he said, "this is what we're going to do. . . ."

FORTY-THREE

Lazarus looked at the two Chinese women. Having to take the two of them was an unexpected complication. He'd only wanted the one girl he had seen with Clint at his hotel, but when he broke into her room, the other girl was with her.

"You're Clint's friend," he had said to her.

"It's me you want," Jenny Soo had said. She looked at Angela Hong, whom she had been trying to counsel, and said, "Let her go."

"I'm sorry," Lazarus had said. He turned to the man with him and said, "Take them both."

Now he looked over at his partner. It was only recently that Lazarus had taken someone on to work with him. He'd almost gotten killed on a recent job, and that made him realize you can't go on alone forever. He looked around for the right man to make his assistant—and someday, his partner—and finally found Mark Kale.

Kale was twenty-eight and, in Lazarus's humble opinion, the man was a born killer. He liked it better than sex—except, the way he was looking at the two Chinese women, maybe sex was what he had on his mind at that moment.

Lazarus looked at the two women again and thought, Why not? It had been hours since he'd had Linda Wentworth.

Clint walked down Dupont Street, which was pitch black at this hour of the night. As much as Jimmy Hong had wanted to come with him, he'd finally convinced him that he should go alone.

He walked to the door that led to the basement. The lock had been broken, probably by Wang and Ki when they had come for the White Powder heads. Idly, Clint wondered where and when the heads would finally surface.

He pushed the door open, pulled his gun, and entered. The broken door swung closed behind him. Inside was no different from outside. It was still pitch black.

He felt for the stone steps with his foot, found them, and started down. He listened intently, hoping to hear something that would help him. He had to figure that Lazarus was not alone. He'd had a man with him when he'd taken the shots at Clint; there was no reason to believe that he wouldn't have him with him now. Although Lazarus's record said he worked alone, a man can always change his working habits.

Clint came to the bottom of the steps and saw a light at the end of the long tunnel. If Lazarus wanted him, he was isolated in that tunnel now. He wondered why no one was on lookout.

He started down the tunnel, moving from one side to the other, moving as quickly as he could, as quietly as he could.

Not quiet enough, though.

He was almost to the end when he heard Lazarus's voice.

"Come and join the party, Adams!" the man said very loudly. His voice echoed.

Clint stopped, then continued on more slowly.

"Of course, there's a slight imbalance," Lazarus went on. "We've got three men and only two women—but that's okay. You can watch what we do with the women before we kill them—and you."

Clint stopped right at the mouth of the tunnel.

"I've got to see your gun come out ahead of you, Adams," Lazarus called out. There was a moment of silence and then Lazarus said, "Now!"

Slowly Clint stuck his hand out, with his gun in it.

"Toss it."

With a flip of his wrist he tossed the gun away.

"Now step out into the open, with your hands where I can see them."

Clint raised his hands, keeping them open, and stepped into the basement. There were candles everywhere, which explained all the light.

Lazarus was standing with his legs spread, a gun in his hand. Behind him Clint saw Jenny Soo and Angela Hong. They were both naked, and another man was standing next to them. He had a gun in his right hand and one of Angela Hong's little breasts in his left. He was grinning.

"Meet Mark Kale," Lazarus said, "my assistant."

That was a surprise—and an unpleasant one.

"Getting old, Lazarus?"

"No," Lazarus said, smiling, "but I want to. You've got to move with the times, Adams. You are alone, I expect?"

"As per your request."

"You work alone, normally, don't you?"

"Most of the time."

"You should consider taking on some help . . . in another life."

"Let the women go, Lazarus," Clint said. "They can't hurt you."

"Oh, but they can hurt *you*," Lazarus said. "I want you to see them die."

"What did I ever do to you?"

"Nothing," Lazarus said. "This is just business."

"You like your business."

"I love it."

"You're doing this one for free, Lazarus."

The man frowned and said, "What do you mean?"

"Your employer is in jail. He can't pay you from there."

"You're lying."

"I'm not," Clint said. "See, his wife's lover tried to kill him, but he shot first."

"Self-defense."

"But the police know he hired you to kill her."

"They can't."

"He told them."

Lazarus shook his head.

"He wouldn't have."

"What I can't figure is why he sent you after me."

Lazarus smiled and said, "I guess you'll never know."

"You can tell me," Clint said. "After all, you are going to kill me, aren't you?"

"Yes," Lazarus said, "I am, and you can wonder all the way to your grave. Good-bye, Adams!"

"Clint!" Jenny Soo shouted.

At that moment a draft entered the room and blew out most of the candles.

"What the—" Lazarus said.

Clint reached behind his back, into his belt, and took out one of the little Colt New Lines.

"Lazarus!" he shouted.

He saw Lazarus's dark shape turn toward him and raise his gun, but Clint fired first. The bullet hit Lazarus in the chest, and he grunted and took a step back.

When the candles went out, Jenny Soo grabbed Angela Hong and yanked her away from Mark Kale.

Lazarus tried to raise his gun again, but Clint fired a second time, putting the second bullet in almost the same place.

McGregor stepped out from the secret passage, with Jimmy Hong behind him. A draft was still at their backs.

"Lazarus!" Mark Kale yelled.

"Here!" McGregor said.

As Kale turned toward the sound of McGregor's voice, the Scotsman fired his gun. The bullet hit Kale just above the right eye, and he dropped.

Lazarus was still trying to bring his gun to bear on Clint, but Clint had closed the distance between them and pulled the man's gun away from him. Somehow Lazarus remained on his feet.

"You're dead, Lazarus," Clint said into his ear. "Fall down."

An eerie cackle rose from the man's throat. He choked on the blood that was filling his lungs, hacked, and then cackled again.

"You'll never know," he said.

"Who cares?" Clint said. He pressed the barrel of the New Line to the man's ear and pulled the trigger. Lazarus's head jerked from the impact of the bullet, and he fell.

Clint turned and, by the dim light of the remaining candles, saw that Jimmy Hong had gathered up both women's clothing and had given it to them. As they dressed, he turned his back.

Maybe he was right. Maybe it wasn't too late for him to play the dutiful brother.

Toy Lee would be pleased.

EPILOGUE

Over coffee in the dining room of the Silver Spur Hotel, Clint tried to help Inspector Alex Saxon understand what had happened.

"I still don't understand," Saxon said, looking at Clint, "why Wentworth sent Lazarus after you."

Clint shrugged.

"I admit I'd like to know why, too, but I can make a couple of guesses."

"Be my guest."

Leona came over with their breakfast, smiled at Clint, and went to take care of another table. When Clint had returned last night—or early this morning—she had not been in his room, so they had not taken care of their unfinished business.

He was looking forward to it.

"Clint?" Saxon said, prodding him.

"Sorry," Clint said. "Well, Mrs. Wentworth came to my room and offered me her lily-white body if I'd tell her what I was doing for her husband."

"And?"

"And maybe he knew she did that, and maybe he thought I took her up on it."

"And?"

"And what?"

"Did you?"

Clint considered not answering, but Saxon had enough unanswered questions.

"No."

He didn't know if Saxon believed him, and he didn't care.

"And what is the other guess?"

"After he hired me he changed his mind," Clint said "By sending Lazarus to 'warn' me he figured I'd take getting fired easier, preferring to lose the job than lose my life. He was trying to scare me off."

"Instead it made you want to stay on the job."

"Right. And after that, he decided to have me killed because I *wouldn't* stop."

Saxon made a face.

"I don't like either one."

"Then get Wentworth to tell you," Clint said.

"Him? He still insists he never heard of a man named Lazarus. Are you sure McGregor will testify?"

Clint nodded. "And so will the two women."

"Yeah, but they're Chinese," Saxon said. "I need McGregor—and you."

"We'll be there."

Saxon stood up, then stared down at Clint.

"Are you sure Lazarus admitted that Wentworth hired him before he died?"

"Dead sure," Clint lied. What the hell, he thought, *he* knew that Wentworth hired Lazarus. He was satisfied with that. A little creative testifying would make sure that Wentworth got what was coming to him—and with him out of the way, Jack Wentworth and Angela Hong could be together.

Of course, there was the little problem of Jack Wentworth not believing that his father was guilty, and blaming Clint for that fact that his father was in prison, but Clint understood that.

He didn't mind having young Wentworth shout obscenities at him at the police station. Angela Hong had come up to him afterward, taken his hand, and promised to talk to Jack.

Clint had better things to worry about than what Jack Wentworth thought of him.

As far as Jimmy Hong was concerned, he had redeemed himself in the eyes of Toy Lee, who felt that maybe the young man was finally ready to grow up and join the family business.

How much of a favor had Clint done Jimmy Hong?

Clint didn't know what would happen with him and Jenny Soo. He also didn't know what was going to happen between him and Leona. Or maybe he did. She did say they had unfinished business. He figured he'd at least have to take the time to say good-bye to both of them properly before he left San Francisco—which wouldn't be for a few days yet, as the game still had that long to run.

"You got lucky last night, Clint," Saxon said, breaking into Clint's reverie.

"Not lucky," Clint said. "I brought in help."

"*That* surprised me. What happened to the lone avenger I know and hate?"

Clint gave Saxon a pitying look and said, "Come on, Inspector. You've got to move with the times."

"Uh, well, yeah, I guess—"

"You find those White Powder Gang heads yet?"

"No, not yet."

"Ah, don't worry," Clint said. "They'll turn up . . . probably where they'll do the most good."

Watch for

THE ROAD TO TESTIMONY

130th in the exciting GUNSMITH series
from Jove

Coming in October!

For the last hundred yards of the stalk, neither man had spoken—not even in whispers—but communicated by signs as they always did when hunting meat to fill hungry bellies. Two steps ahead, George Drewyer, the man recognized to be the best hunter in the Lewis and Clark party, sank down on his right knee, froze, and peered intently through the glistening wet bushes and dangling evergreen tree limbs toward the animal grazing in the clearing. Identifying it, he turned, using his hands swiftly and graphically to tell the younger, less experienced hunter, Matt Crane, the nature of the animal he had seen and how he meant to approach and kill it.

Not a deer, his hands said. Not an elk. Just a stray Indian horse—with no Indians in sight. He'd move up on it from downwind, his hands said, until he got into sure-kill range, then he'd put a ball from his long rifle into its head. What he expected Matt to do was follow a couple of steps behind and a few feet off to the right, stopping when he stopped, aiming when he aimed, but firing only if the actions of the horse clearly showed that Drewyer's ball had missed.

Matt signed that he understood. Turning back toward the clearing, George Drewyer began his final stalk.

Underfoot, the leaf mold and fallen pine needles formed a yielding carpet beneath the scattered clumps of bushes and thick stands of pines, which here on the western slope of the Bitter Root Mountains were broader in girth and taller than the skinny lodgepole and larch found on the higher reaches of the Lolo Trail. Half a day's travel behind, the other thirty-two members of the party still were struggling in foot-deep snow over slick rocks, steep slides, and tangles of down timber treacherous as logjams, as they sought the headwaters of the Columbia and the final segment of their journey to the Pacific Ocean.

It had been four days since the men had eaten meat, Matt knew, being forced to sustain themselves on the detested army ration called "portable soup," a grayish brown jelly that looked like a mixture of pulverized wood duff and dried dung, tasted like iron filings, and even when flavored with meat drippings and dissolved in hot water satisfied the belly no more than a swallow of air. Nor had the last solid food been much, for the foal butchered at Colt-Killed Creek had been dropped by its dam only a few months ago; though its meat was tender enough, most of its growth had gone into muscle and bone, its immature carcass making skimpy portions when distributed among such a large party of famished men.

With September only half gone, winter had already come to the seven-thousand-foot-high backbone of the continent a week's travel behind. All the game that the old Shoshone guide, Toby, had told them usually was to be found in the high meadows at this time of year had moved down to lower levels. Desperate for food, Captain William Clark had sent George Drewyer and Matt Crane scouting ahead for meat, judging that two men traveling afoot and unencumbered would stand a much better chance of finding game than the main party with its thirty-odd men and twenty-nine heavily laden horses. As he usually did, Drewyer had found game of a sort, weighed the risk of rousing the hostility of its Indian owner against the need of the party for food, and decided that hunger recognized no property rights.

In the drizzling cold rain, the coat of the grazing horse glistened like polished metal. It would be around four years old, Matt guessed, a brown and white paint, well muscled, sleek, alert. If this were a typical Nez Perce horse, he could well believe what the Shoshone chief, Cameahwait, had told Captain Clark—that the finest horses to be found in this part of the country were those raised by the Shoshones' mortal enemies, the Nez Perces. Viewing such a handsome animal cropping bluegrass on a Missouri hillside eighteen months ago, Matt Crane would have itched to rope, saddle, and ride it, testing its speed, wind, and spirit. Now all he itched to do was kill and eat it.

Twenty paces away from the horse, which still was grazing placidly, George Drewyer stopped, knelt behind a fallen tree, soundlessly rested the barrel of his long rifle on its trunk, and took careful aim. Two steps to his right, Matt Crane did the same. After what seemed an agonizingly long period of time, during which Matt held his breath, Drewyer's rifle barked. Without movement or sound, the paint horse sank to the ground, dead—Matt was sure—before its body touched the sodden earth.

"Watch it!" Drewyer murmured, swiftly reversing his rifle, swabbing out its barrel with the ramrod, expertly reloading it with patched and greased lead ball, wiping flint and firing hammer clean, then opening the pan and pouring in a carefully measured charge while he protected it from the drizzle with the tree trunk and his body.

Keeping his own rifle sighted on the fallen horse, Matt held his position without moving or speaking, as George Drewyer had taught him to do, until the swarthy, dark-eyed hunter had reloaded his weapon and risen to one knee. Peering first at the still animal, then moving his searching gaze around the clearing, Drewyer tested the immediate environment with all his senses—sight, sound, smell, and his innate hunter's instinct—for a full minute before he at last nodded in satisfaction.

"A bunch-quitter, likely. Least there's no herd nor herders around. Think you can skin it, preacher boy?"

"Sure. You want it quartered, with the innards saved in the hide?"

"Just like we'd do with an elk. Save everything but the hoofs and whinny. Get at it, while I snoop around for Injun sign. The Nez Perces will be friendly, the captains say, but I'd as soon not meet the Injun that owned that horse till its head and hide are out of sight."

While George Drewyer circled the clearing and prowled through the timber beyond, Matt Crane went to the dead horse, unsheathed his butcher knife, skillfully made the cuts needed to strip off the hide, and gutted and dissected the animal. Returning from his scout, Drewyer hunkered down beside him, quickly boned out as large a packet of choice cuts as he could conveniently carry, wrapped them in a piece of hide, and loaded the still-warm meat into the empty canvas backpack he had brought along for that purpose.

"It ain't likely the men'll get this far by dark," he said, "so I'll take 'em a taste to ease their bellies for the night. Can you make out alone till tomorrow noon?"

"Yes."

"From what I seen, the timber thins out a mile or so ahead. Seems to be a kind of open, marshy prairie beyond, which is where the Nez Perces come this time of year to dig roots, Toby says. Drag the head and hide back in the bushes out of sight. Cut the meat up into pieces you can spit and broil, then build a fire and start it cooking. If the smoke and smell brings Injun company, give 'em the peace sign, invite 'em to sit and eat, and tell 'em a big party of white men will be coming down the trail tomorrow. You got all that, preacher boy?"

"Yes."

"Good. Give me a hand with this pack and I'll be on my way." Slipping his arms through the straps and securing the pad that transferred a portion of the weight to his forehead, Drewyer got to his feet while Matt Crane eased the load. Grinning, Drewyer squeezed his shoulder. "Remind me to quit calling you preacher boy, will you, Matt? You've learned a lot since you left home."

"I've had a good teacher."

"That you have! Take care."

Left alone in the whispering silence of the forest and the cold, mist-like rain, Matt Crane dragged the severed head and hide into a clump of nearby bushes. Taking his hatchet, he searched for and found enough resinous wood, bark, and dry duff to catch the spark from his flint and steel. As the fire grew in the narrow trench he had dug for it, he cut forked sticks, placed pieces of green aspen limbs horizontally across them, sliced the meat into strips, and started it to broiling. The smell of juice dripping into the fire made his belly churn with hunger, tempting him to do what Touissant Charbonneau, the party's French-Canadian interpreter, did when fresh-killed game was brought into camp—seize a hunk and gobble it down hot, raw, and bloody. But he did not, preferring to endure the piercing hunger pangs just a little longer in exchange for the greater pleasure of savoring his first bite of well-cooked meat.

Cutting more wood for the fire, he hoped George Drewyer would stop calling him "preacher boy." Since at twenty he was one of the youngest members of the party and his father, the Reverend Peter Crane, was a Presbyterian minister in St. Louis, it had been natural enough for the older men to call him "the preacher's boy" at first. Among a less disciplined band, he would have been forced to endure a good deal of hoorawing and would have been the butt of many practical jokes. But the no-nonsense military leadership of the two captains put strict limits on that sort of thing.

Why Drewyer—who'd been raised a Catholic, could barely read and write, and had no peer as an outdoorsman—should have made Matt his protégé, Matt himself could not guess. Maybe because he was malleable, did what he was told to do, and never backed off from hard work. Maybe because he listened more than he talked. Or maybe because he was having the adventure of his life and showed it. Whatever the reason, their relationship was good. It would be even better,

Matt mused, if Drewyer would drop the "preacher boy" thing and simply call him by name.

While butchering the horse, Matt noticed that it had been gelded as a colt. According to George Drewyer, the Nez Perces were one of the few Western Indian tribes that practiced selective breeding, thus the high quality of their horses. From the way Chief Cameahwait had acted, a state of war existed between the Shoshones and the Nez Perces, so the first contact between the Lewis and Clark party—which had passed through Shoshone country—and the Nez Perces was going to be fraught with danger. Aware of the fact that he might make the first contact, Matt Crane felt both uneasy and proud. Leaving him alone in this area showed the confidence Drewyer had in him. But his aloneness made him feel a little spooky.

With the afternoon only half gone and nothing to do but tend the fire, Matt stashed his blanket roll under a tree out of the wet, picked up his rifle, and curiously studied the surrounding forest. There was no discernible wind, but vagrant currents of air stirred, bringing to his nostrils the smell of wood smoke, of crushed pine needles, of damp leaf mold, of burnt black powder. As he moved across the clearing toward a three-foot-wide stream gurgling down the slope, he scowled, suddenly realizing that the burnt black powder smell could not have lingered behind this long. Nor would it have gotten stronger, as this smell was doing the nearer he came to the stream. Now he identified it beyond question.

Sulfur! There must be a mineral-impregnated hot spring nearby, similar to the hot springs near Traveler's Rest at the eastern foot of Lolo Pass, where the cold, weary members of the party had eased their aches and pains in warm, soothing pools. What he wouldn't give for a hot bath right now!

At the edge of the stream, he knelt, dipping his hand into the water. It was warm. Cupping his palm, he tasted it, finding it strongly sulfurous. If this were like the stream on the other side of the mountains, he mused, there would be one or more scalding, heavily impregnated springs issuing from old volcanic rocks higher up the slope, their waters diluted by colder side rivulets joining the main stream, making it simply a matter of exploration to find water temperature and a chemical content best suited to the needs of a cold, tired body. The prospect intrigued him.

Visually checking the meat broiling over the fire, he judged it could do without tending for an hour or so. Thick though the forest cover was along the sides of the stream, he would run no risk of getting lost, for following the stream downhill would bring him back to the clearing. Time enough then to cut limbs for a lean-to and rig a shelter for the night.

Sometimes wading in the increasingly warm waters of the stream, sometimes on its bush-bordered bank, he followed its windings uphill for half a mile before he found what he was looking for: a pool ten feet long and half as wide, eroded in smooth basalt, ranging in depth from one to four feet. Testing the temperature of its water, he found it just right—hot but not unbearably so, the sulfur smell strong but not unpleasant. Leaning his rifle against a tree trunk, he took off his limp, shapeless red felt hat, pulled his thin moccasins off his bruised and swollen feet, waded into the pool, and gasped with sensual pleasure as the heat of the water spread upward.

Since his fringed buckskin jacket and woolen trousers already were soaking wet from the cold rain, he kept them on as he first sank to a sitting position, then stretched out full length on his back, with only his head above water. After a time, he roused himself long enough to strip the jacket off over his head and pull the trousers down over his ankles. Tossing them into a clump of bushes near his rifle, hat, and moccasins, he lay back in the soothing water, naked, warm, and comfortable for the first time since Traveler's Rest.

Drowsily, his eyes closed. He slept . . .

The sound that awakened him some time later could have been made by a deer moving down to drink from the pool just upstream from where he lay. It could have been made by a beaver searching for a choice willow sapling to cut down. It could have been made by a bobcat, a bear, or a cougar. But as consciousness returned to him, as he heard the sound and attempted to identify it, his intelligence rejected each possibility that occurred to him the moment it crossed his mind—for one lucid reason.

Animals did not sing. And whatever this intruder into his state of tranquillity might be, it was singing.

Though the words were not recognizable, they had an Indian sound, unmistakably conveying the message that the singer was at peace with the world, not self-conscious, and about to indulge in a very enjoyable act. Turning over on his belly, Matt crawled to the upper end of the pool, peering through the screening bushes in the direction from which the singing sound was coming. The light was poor. Even so, it was good enough for him to make out the figure of a girl, standing in profile not ten feet away, reaching down to the hem of her buckskin skirt, lifting it, and pulling it up over her head.

As she tossed the garment aside, she turned, momentarily facing him. His first thought was *My God, she's beautiful!* His second: *She's naked!* His third: *How can I get away from here without being seen?*

That she was not aware of his presence was made clear enough by the fact that she still was crooning her bath-taking song, her gaze intent on her footing as she stepped gingerly into a pool just a few yards upstream from the one in which he lay. Though he had stopped breathing for fear she would hear the sound, he could not justify leaving his eyes open for fear she would hear the lids closing. Morally wrong though he knew it was to stare at her, he could not even blink or look away.

She would be around sixteen years old, he judged, her skin light copper in color, her mouth wide and generous, with dimples indenting both cheeks. Her breasts were full but not heavy; her waist was slim, her stomach softly rounded, her hips beginning to broaden with maturity, her legs long and graceful. Watching her sink slowly into the water until only the tips of her breasts and her head were exposed, Matt felt no guilt for continuing to stare at her. Instead he mused, *So that's what a naked woman looks like! Why should I be ashamed to admire such beauty?*

He began breathing again, careful to make no sound. Since the two pools were no more than a dozen feet apart, separated by a thin screen of bushes and a short length of stream, which here made only a faint gurgling noise, he knew that getting out of the water, retrieving his clothes and rifle, and then withdrawing from the vicinity without revealing his presence would require utmost caution. But the attempt must be made, for if one young Indian woman knew of this bathing spot, others must know of it, too, and in all likelihood soon would be coming here to join her.

He could well imagine his treatment at their hands, if found. Time and again recently the two captains had warned members of the party that Western Indians such as the Shoshones, Flatheads, and Nez Perces had a far higher standard of morality than did the Mandans, with whom the party had wintered, who would gladly sell the favor of wives and daughters for a handful of beads, a piece of bright cloth, or a cheap trade knife, and cheerfully provide shelter and bed for the act.

Moving with infinite care, he half floated, half crawled to the lower right-hand edge of the pool, where he had left his rifle and clothes. The Indian girl still was singing. The bank was steep and slick. Standing up, he took hold of a sturdy-feeling, thumb-thick sapling rooted near the edge of the bank, cautiously tested it, and judged it secure. Pulling himself out of the pool, he started to take a step, slipped, and tried to save himself by grabbing the sapling with both hands.

The full weight of his body proved too much for its root system. Torn out of the wet earth, it no longer supported him. As he fell backward into the pool, he gave an involuntary cry of disgust.

"Oh, shit!"

Underwater, his mouth, nose, and eyes filled as he struggled to turn over and regain his footing. When he did so,

he immediately became aware of the fact that the girl had
stopped singing. Choking, coughing up water, half-blinded,
and completely disoriented, he floundered out of the pool
toward where he thought his clothes and rifle were. Seeing
a garment draped over a bush, he grabbed it, realized it was
not his, hastily turned away, and blundered squarely into a wet,
naked body.

To save themselves from falling, both he and the Indian
girl clung to each other momentarily. She began screaming.
Hastily he let her go. Still screaming and staring at him with
terror-stricken eyes, she snatched her dress off the bush and
held it so that it covered her. Finding his own clothes, he held
them in front of his body, trying to calm the girl by making
the sign for "friend," "white man," and "peace," while urgently
saying:

"*Ta-ba-bone,* you understand? *Suyapo!* I went to sleep, you
see, and had no idea you were around . . ."

Suddenly her screaming stopped. Not because of his words
or hand signs, Matt feared, but because of the appearance of
an Indian man who had pushed through the bushes and now
stood beside her. He was dressed in beaded, fringed buckskins,
was stocky, slightly bowlegged, a few inches shorter than Matt
but more muscular and heavier, a man in his middle twenties,
with high cheekbones and a firm jawline. He shot a guttural
question at the girl, to which she replied in a rapid babble
of words. His dark brown eyes blazed with anger. Drawing
a glittering knife out of its sheath, he motioned the girl to step
aside, and moved toward Matt menacingly.

Backing away, Matt thought frantically, *Captain Clark is not
going to like this at all. And if that Indian does what it looks
like he means to do with that knife, I'm not going to like it,
either . . .*

J.R. ROBERTS
THE
GUNSMITH

AUG 2 5 '92 BAS